Bloodchild

and Other Stories

SECOND EDITION

Also by Octavia E. Butler

Patternmaster
Mind of My Mind
Survivor
Kindred
Wild Seed
Clay's Ark
Dawn
Adulthood Rites
Imago
Parable of the Sower
Parable of the Talents
Fledgling

Bloodchild
and Other Stories

SECOND EDITION

Octavia E. Butler

SEVEN STORIES PRESS
New York

Published by
Seven Stories Press
140 Watts Street
New York, NY 10013
www.sevenstories.com

Library of Congress Cataloging-in-Publication Data

Butler, Octavia E.
Bloodchild and other stories / Octavia E. Butler.-- 2nd ed.
p. cm.
ISBN: 978-1-58322-698-8 (pbk. : alk. paper)
1. Science fiction, American. 2. Women--Fiction. I. Title.
PS3552.U827A6 2005
813'.54--dc22
2005018898

College professors may order examination copies of Seven Stories Press titles for a free six-month trial period. To order, visit www.sevenstories.com/textbook/ or send a fax on school letterhead to 212.226.1411.

Printed in the USA.
Book design by Acme Art, Inc.

18 17

-Contents-

Preface

The truth is, I hate short story writing. Trying to do it has taught me much more about frustration and despair than I ever wanted to know.

Yet there is something seductive about writing short stories. It looks so easy. You come up with an idea, then ten, twenty, perhaps thirty pages later, you've got a finished story.

Well, maybe.

My earliest collections of pages weren't stories at all. They were fragments of longer works—of stalled, unfinished novels. Or they were brief summaries of unwritten novels. Or they were isolated incidents that could not stand alone.

All that, and poorly written, too.

It didn't help that my college writing teachers said only polite, lukewarm things about them. They couldn't help me much with the science fiction and fantasy I kept turning out. In fact, they didn't have a very high opinion of anything that could be called science fiction.

Editors regularly rejected my stories, returning them with the familiar, unsigned, printed rejection slips. This, of course, was the writer's rite of passage. I knew it, but that didn't make it easier. And as for short stories, I used to give up writing them the way some people give up smoking cigarettes—over and over again. I couldn't escape my story ideas, and I couldn't make them work as short stories. After a long struggle, I made some of them work as novels.

Which is what they should have been all along.

I am essentially a novelist. The ideas that most interest me tend to be big. Exploring them takes more time and space than a short story can contain.

And yet, every now and then one of my short stories really is a short story. The five stories in this collection really are short stories. I've never been tempted to turn them into novels. This book, however, has tempted me to add to them—not to make them longer, but to talk about each of them. I've included a brief afterword with each story. I like the idea of afterwords rather than individual introductions since afterwords allow me to talk freely about the stories without ruining them for readers. It will be a pleasure to make use of such freedom. Before now, other people have done all the print interpretations of my work: "Butler seems to be saying . . ." "Obviously, Butler believes . . ." "Butler makes it clear that she feels . . ."

Actually, I feel that what people bring to my work is at least as important to them as what I put into it. But I'm still glad to be able to talk a little about what I do put into my work, and what it means to me.

-Stories-

Bloodchild

My last night of childhood began with a visit home. T'Gatoi's sister had given us two sterile eggs. T'Gatoi gave one to my mother, brother, and sisters. She insisted that I eat the other one alone. It didn't matter. There was still enough to leave everyone feeling good. Almost everyone. My mother wouldn't take any. She sat, watching everyone drifting and dreaming without her. Most of the time she watched me.

I lay against T'Gatoi's long, velvet underside, sipping from my egg now and then, wondering why my mother denied herself such a harmless pleasure. Less of her hair would be gray if she indulged now and then. The eggs prolonged life, prolonged vigor. My father, who had never refused one in his life, had lived more than twice as long as he should have. And toward the end of his life, when he should have been slowing down, he had married my mother and fathered four children.

But my mother seemed content to age before she had to. I saw her turn away as several of T'Gatoi's limbs secured me closer. T'Gatoi liked our body heat and took advantage of it whenever she could. When I was little and at home more, my mother used to try to tell me how to behave with T'Gatoi—how to be respectful and always obedient because T'Gatoi was the Tlic government official in charge of the Preserve, and thus the most important of her kind to deal directly with Terrans.

It was an honor, my mother said, that such a person had chosen to come into the family. My mother was at her most formal and severe when she was lying.

I had no idea why she was lying, or even what she was lying about. It *was* an honor to have T'Gatoi in the family, but it was hardly a novelty. T'Gatoi and my mother had been friends all my mother's life, and T'Gatoi was not interested in being honored in the house she considered her second home. She simply came in, climbed onto one of her special couches, and called me over to keep her warm. It was impossible to be formal with her while lying against her and hearing her complain as usual that I was too skinny.

"You're better," she said this time, probing me with six or seven of her limbs. "You're gaining weight finally. Thinness is dangerous." The probing changed subtly, became a series of caresses.

"He's still too thin," my mother said sharply.

T'Gatoi lifted her head and perhaps a meter of her body off the couch as though she were sitting up. She looked at my mother, and my mother, her face lined and old looking, turned away.

"Lien, I would like you to have what's left of Gan's egg."

"The eggs are for the children," my mother said.

"They are for the family. Please take it."

Unwillingly obedient, my mother took it from me and put it to her mouth. There were only a few drops left in the now-shrunken, elastic shell, but she squeezed them out, swallowed them, and after a few moments some of the lines of tension began to smooth from her face.

"It's good," she whispered. "Sometimes I forget how good it is."

"You should take more," T'Gatoi said. "Why are you in such a hurry to be old?"

My mother said nothing.

"I like being able to come here," T'Gatoi said. "This place is a refuge because of you, yet you won't take care of yourself."

T'Gatoi was hounded on the outside. Her people wanted more of us made available. Only she and her political faction stood between us and the hordes who did not understand why there was a Preserve—why any Terran could not be courted, paid, drafted, in some way made available to them. Or they did understand, but in their desperation, they did not care. She parceled us out to the desperate and sold us to the rich and powerful for their political support. Thus, we were necessities, status symbols, and an independent people. She oversaw the joining of families, putting an end to the final remnants of the earlier system of breaking up Terran families to suit impatient Tlic. I had lived outside with her. I had seen the desperate eagerness in the way some people looked at me. It was a little frightening to know that only she stood between us and that desperation that could so easily swallow us. My mother would look at her sometimes and say to me, "Take care of her." And I would remember that she too had been outside, had seen.

Now T'Gatoi used four of her limbs to push me away from her onto the floor. "Go on, Gan," she said. "Sit down there with your sisters and enjoy not being sober. You had most of the egg. Lien, come warm me."

My mother hesitated for no reason that I could see. One of my earliest memories is of my mother stretched alongside T'Gatoi, talking about things I could not understand, picking me up from the floor and laughing as she sat me on one of T'Gatoi's segments. She ate her share of eggs then. I wondered when she had stopped, and why.

She lay down now against T'Gatoi, and the whole left row of T'Gatoi's limbs closed around her, holding her loosely, but securely. I had always found it comfortable to lie that way, but except for my older sister, no one else in the family liked it. They said it made them feel caged.

T'Gatoi meant to cage my mother. Once she had, she moved her tail slightly, then spoke. "Not enough egg, Lien. You should have taken it when it was passed to you. You need it badly now."

T'Gatoi's tail moved once more, its whip motion so swift I wouldn't have seen it if I hadn't been watching for it. Her sting drew only a single drop of blood from my mother's bare leg.

My mother cried out—probably in surprise. Being stung doesn't hurt. Then she sighed and I could see her body relax. She moved languidly into a more comfortable position within the cage of T'Gatoi's limbs. "Why did you do that?" she asked, sounding half asleep.

"I could not watch you sitting and suffering any longer."

My mother managed to move her shoulders in a small shrug. "Tomorrow," she said.

"Yes. Tomorrow you will resume your suffering—if you must. But just now, just for now, lie here and warm me and let me ease your way a little."

"He's still mine, you know," my mother said suddenly.

"Nothing can buy him from me." Sober, she would not have permitted herself to refer to such things.

"Nothing," T'Gatoi agreed, humoring her.

"Did you think I would sell him for eggs? For long life? My son?"

"Not for anything," T'Gatoi said, stroking my mother's shoulders, toying with her long, graying hair.

I would like to have touched my mother, shared that moment with her. She would take my hand if I touched her now. Freed by the egg and the sting, she would smile and perhaps say things long held in. But tomorrow, she would remember all this as a humiliation. I did not want to be part of a remembered humiliation. Best just be still and know she loved me under all the duty and pride and pain.

"Xuan Hoa, take off her shoes," T'Gatoi said. "In a little while I'll sting her again and she can sleep."

My older sister obeyed, swaying drunkenly as she stood up. When she had finished, she sat down beside me and took my hand. We had always been a unit, she and I.

My mother put the back of her head against T'Gatoi's underside and tried from that impossible angle to look up into the broad, round face. "You're going to sting me again?"

"Yes, Lien."

"I'll sleep until tomorrow noon."

"Good. You need it. When did you sleep last?"

My mother made a wordless sound of annoyance. "I should have stepped on you when you were small enough," she muttered.

It was an old joke between them. They had grown up together, sort of, though T'Gatoi had not, in my mother's lifetime, been small enough for any Terran to step on. She was nearly three time my mother's present age, yet would still be young when my mother died of age. But T'Gatoi and my mother had met as T'Gatoi was coming into a period of rapid development—a kind of Tlic adolescence. My mother was only a child, but for a while they developed at the same rate and had no better friends than each other.

T'Gatoi had even introduced my mother to the man who became my father. My parents, pleased with each other in spite of their different ages, married as T'Gatoi was going into her family's business—politics. She and my mother saw each other less. But sometime before my older sister was born, my mother promised T'Gatoi one of her children. She would have to give one of us to someone, and she preferred T'Gatoi to some stranger.

Years passed. T'Gatoi traveled and increased her influence. The Preserve was hers by the time she came back to my mother to collect what she probably saw as her just reward for her hard work. My older sister took an instant liking to her and wanted to be chosen, but my mother was just coming to term with me and T'Gatoi liked the idea of choosing an infant and watching and taking part in all the phases of development. I'm told I was first caged within T'Gatoi's many limbs only three minutes after my birth. A few days later, I was given my first taste of egg. I tell Terrans that when they ask whether I was ever afraid of her. And I tell it to Tlic when T'Gatoi suggests a young Terran child for them and they, anxious and ignorant, demand an adolescent. Even my brother who had somehow grown up to fear and distrust the Tlic could probably have gone smoothly into one of their families if he had been adopted early enough. Sometimes, I think for his sake he should have been. I looked at him, stretched out on the floor across the room, his eyes open, but glazed as he dreamed his egg dream. No matter what he felt toward the Tlic, he always demanded his share of egg.

"Lien, can you stand up?" T'Gatoi asked suddenly.

"Stand?" my mother said. "I thought I was going to sleep."

"Later. Something sounds wrong outside." The cage was abruptly gone.

"What?"

"Up, Lien!"

My mother recognized her tone and got up just in time to avoid being dumped on the floor. T'Gatoi whipped her three meters of body off her couch, toward the door, and out at full speed. She had bones—ribs, a long spine, a skull, four sets of limb bones per segment. But when she moved that way, twisting, hurling herself into controlled falls, landing running, she seemed not only boneless, but aquatic—something swimming through the air as though it were water. I loved watching her move.

I left my sister and started to follow her out the door, though I wasn't very steady on my own feet. It would have been better to sit and dream, better yet to find a girl and share a waking dream with her. Back when the Tlic saw us as not much more than convenient, big, warm-blooded animals, they would pen several of us together, male and female, and feed us only eggs. That way they could be sure of getting another generation of us no matter how we tried to hold out. We were lucky that didn't go on long. A few generations of it and we would have *been* little more than convenient, big animals.

"Hold the door open, Gan," T'Gatoi said. "And tell the family to stay back."

"What is it?" I asked.

"N'Tlic."

I shrank back against the door. "Here? Alone?"

"He was trying to reach a call box, I suppose." She carried the man past me, unconscious, folded like a coat over some of her limbs. He looked young—my brother's age perhaps—and he was thinner than he should have been. What T'Gatoi would have called dangerously thin.

"Gan, go to the call box," she said. She put the man on the floor and began stripping off his clothing.

I did not move.

After a moment, she looked up at me, her sudden stillness a sign of deep impatience.

"Send Qui," I told her. "I'll stay here. Maybe I can help."

She let her limbs begin to move again, lifting the man and pulling his shirt over his head. "You don't want to see this," she said. "It will be hard. I can't help this man the way his Tlic could."

"I know. But send Qui. He won't want to be of any help here. I'm at least willing to try."

She looked at my brother—older, bigger, stronger, certainly more able to help her here. He was sitting up now, braced against the wall, staring at the man on the floor with undisguised fear and revulsion. Even she could see that he would be useless.

"Qui, go!" she said.

He didn't argue. He stood up, swayed briefly, then steadied, frightened sober.

"This man's name is Bram Lomas," she told him, reading from the man's armband. I fingered my own armband in sympathy. "He needs T'Khotgif Teh. Do you hear?"

"Bram Lomas, T'Khotgif Teh," my brother said. "I'm going." He edged around Lomas and ran out the door.

Lomas began to regain consciousness. He only moaned at first and clutched spasmodically at a pair of T'Gatoi's limbs. My younger sister, finally awake from her egg dream, came close to look at him, until my mother pulled her back.

T'Gatoi removed the man's shoes, then his pants, all the while leaving him two of her limbs to grip. Except for the final few, all her limbs were equally dexterous. "I want no argument from you this time, Gan," she said.

I straightened. "What shall I do?"

"Go out and slaughter an animal that is at least half your size."

"Slaughter? But I've never —"

She knocked me across the room. Her tail was an efficient weapon whether she exposed the sting or not.

I got up, feeling stupid for having ignored her warning, and went into the kitchen. Maybe I could kill something with a knife or an ax. My mother raised a few Terran animals for the table and several thousand local ones for their fur. T'Gatoi would probably prefer something local. An achti, perhaps. Some of those were the right size, though they had about three times as many teeth as I did and a real love of using them. My mother, Hoa, and Qui could kill them with knives. I had never killed one at all, had never slaughtered any animal. I had spent most of my time with T'Gatoi while my brother and sisters were learning the family business. T'Gatoi had been right. I should have been the one to go to the call box. At least I could do that.

I went to the corner cabinet where my mother kept her large house and garden tools. At the back of the cabinet there was a pipe that carried off waste water from the kitchen—except that it didn't anymore. My father had rerouted the waste water below before I was born. Now the pipe could be turned so that one half slid around the other and a rifle could be stored inside. This wasn't our only gun, but it was our most easily accessible one. I would have to use it to shoot one of the biggest of the achti. Then T'Gatoi would probably confiscate it. Firearms were illegal in the Preserve. There had been incidents right after the Preserve was established—Terrans shooting Tlic, shooting N'Tlic. This was before the joining of families began, before everyone had a personal stake in keeping the peace. No one had shot a Tlic in my lifetime or my mother's, but the law still stood—for our protection, we were told. There were stories of whole Terran families wiped out in reprisal back during the assassinations.

I went out to the cages and shot the biggest achti I could find. It was a handsome breeding male, and my mother would not be pleased to see me bring it in. But it was the right size, and I was in a hurry.

I put the achti's long, warm body over my shoulder—glad that some of the weight I'd gained was muscle—and took it to the kitchen. There, I put the gun back in its hiding place. If T'Gatoi noticed the achti's wounds and demanded the gun, I would give it to her. Otherwise, let it stay where my father wanted it.

I turned to take the achti to her, then hesitated. For several seconds, I stood in front of the closed door wondering why I was suddenly afraid. I knew what was going to happen. I hadn't seen it before but T'Gatoi had shown me diagrams and drawings. She had made sure I knew the truth as soon as I was old enough to understand it.

Yet I did not want to go into that room. I wasted a little time choosing a knife from the carved, wooden box in which my mother kept them. T'Gatoi might want one, I told myself, for the tough, heavily furred hide of the achti.

"Gan!" T'Gatoi called, her voice harsh with urgency.

I swallowed. I had not imagined a single moving of the feet could be so difficult. I realized I was trembling and that shamed me. Shame impelled me through the door.

I put the achti down near T'Gatoi and saw that Lomas was unconscious again. She, Lomas, and I were alone in the room—my mother and sisters probably sent out so they would not have to watch. I envied them.

But my mother came back into the room as T'Gatoi seized the achti. Ignoring the knife I offered her, she extended claws from several of her limbs and slit the achti from throat to anus. She looked at me, her yellow eyes intent. "Hold this man's shoulders, Gan."

I stared at Lomas in panic, realizing that I did not want to touch him, let alone hold him. This would not be like shooting an animal. Not as quick, not as merciful, and, I hoped, not as final, but there was nothing I wanted less than to be part of it.

My mother came forward. "Gan, you hold his right side," she said. "I'll hold his left." And if he came to, he would throw her off without realizing he had done it. She was a tiny woman. She often wondered aloud how she had produced, as she said, such "huge" children.

"Never mind," I told her, taking the man's shoulders. "I'll do it." She hovered nearby.

"Don't worry," I said. "I won't shame you. You don't have to stay and watch."

She looked at me uncertainly, then touched my face in a rare caress. Finally, she went back to her bedroom.

T'Gatoi lowered her head in relief. "Thank you, Gan," she said with courtesy more Terran than Tlic. "That one . . . she is always finding new ways for me to make her suffer."

Lomas began to groan and make choked sounds. I had hoped he would stay unconscious. T'Gatoi put her face near his so that he focused on her.

"I've stung you as much as I dare for now," she told him. "When this is over, I'll sting you to sleep and you won't hurt anymore."

"Please," the man begged. "Wait . . . "

"There's no more time, Bram. I'll sting you as soon as it's over. When T'Khotgif arrives she'll give you eggs to help you heal. It will be over soon."

"T'Khotgif!" the man shouted, straining against my hands.

"Soon, Bram." T'Gatoi glanced at me, then placed a claw against his abdomen slightly to the right of the middle, just below the left rib. There was movement on the right side—tiny, seemingly random pulsations moving his brown flesh, creating a concavity here, a convexity there, over and over until I could see the rhythm of it and knew where the next pulse would be.

Lomas's entire body stiffened under T'Gatoi's claw, though she merely rested it against him as she wound the rear section of her body around his legs. He might break my grip, but he would not break hers. He wept helplessly as she used his pants to tie his hands, then pushed his hands above his head so that I could kneel on the cloth between them and pin them in place. She rolled up his shirt and gave it to him to bite down on.

And she opened him.

His body convulsed with the first cut. He almost tore himself away from me. The sound he made . . . I had never heard such sounds come from anything human. T'Gatoi seemed to pay no attention as she lengthened and deepened the cut, now and then pausing to lick away blood. His blood vessels contracted, reacting to the chemistry of her saliva, and the bleeding slowed.

I felt as though I were helping her torture him, helping her consume him. I knew I would vomit soon, didn't know why I hadn't already. I couldn't possibly last until she was finished.

She found the first grub. It was fat and deep red with his blood—both inside and out. It had already eaten its own egg case but apparently had not yet begun to eat its host. At this stage, it would eat any flesh except its mother's. Let alone, it would have gone on excreting the poisons that had both sickened and alerted Lomas. Eventually it would have begun to eat. By the time it ate its way out of Lomas's flesh, Lomas would be dead or dying—and unable to take revenge on the thing that was killing him. There was always a grace period between the time the host sickened and the time the grubs began to eat him.

T'Gatoi picked up the writhing grub carefully and looked at it, somehow ignoring the terrible groans of the man.

Abruptly, the man lost consciousness.

"Good," T'Gatoi looked down at him. "I wish you Terrans could do that at will." She felt nothing. And the thing she held . . .

It was limbless and boneless at this stage, perhaps fifteen centimeters long and two thick, blind and slimy with blood. It was like a large worm. T'Gatoi put it into the belly of the achti, and it began at once to burrow. It would stay there and eat as long as there was anything to eat.

Probing through Lomas's flesh, she found two more, one of them smaller and more vigorous. "A male!" she said happily. He would be dead before I would. He would be through his metamorphosis and screwing everything that would hold still before his sisters even had limbs. He was the only one to make a serious effort to bite T'Gatoi as she placed him in the achti.

Paler worms oozed to visibility in Lomas's flesh. I closed my eyes. It was worse than finding something dead, rotting, and filled with tiny animal grubs. And it was far worse than any drawing or diagram.

"Ah, there are more," T'Gatoi said, plucking out two long, thick grubs. You may have to kill another animal, Gan. Everything lives inside you Terrans."

I had been told all my life that this was a good and necessary thing Tlic and Terran did together—a kind of birth. I had believed it until now. I knew birth was painful and bloody, no matter what. But this was something else, something worse. And I wasn't ready to see it. Maybe I never would be. Yet I couldn't not see it. Closing my eyes didn't help.

T'Gatoi found a grub still eating its egg case. The remains of the case were still wired into a blood vessel by their own little tube or hook or whatever. That was the way the grubs were anchored and the way they fed. They took only blood until they were ready to emerge. Then they ate their stretched, elastic egg cases. Then they ate their hosts.

T'Gatoi bit away the egg case, licked away the blood. Did she like the taste? Did childhood habits die hard—or not die at all?

The whole procedure was wrong, alien. I wouldn't have thought anything about her could seem alien to me.

"One more, I think," she said. "Perhaps two. A good family. In a host animal these days, we would be happy to find one or two alive." She glanced at me. "Go outside, Gan, and empty your stomach. Go now while the man is unconscious."

I staggered out, barely made it. Beneath the tree just beyond the front door, I vomited until there was nothing left to bring up. Finally, I stood shaking, tears streaming down my face. I did not know why I was crying, but I could not stop. I went further from the house to avoid being seen. Every time I closed my eyes I saw red worms crawling over redder human flesh.

There was a car coming toward the house. Since Terrans were forbidden motorized vehicles except for certain farm equipment, I knew this must be Lomas's Tlic with Qui and perhaps a Terran doctor. I wiped my face on my shirt, struggled for control.

"Gan," Qui called as the car stopped. "What happened?" He crawled out of the low, round, Tlic-convenient car door. Another Terran crawled out the other side and went into the house without speaking to me. The doctor. With his help and a few eggs, Lomas might make it.

"T'Khotgif Teh?" I said.

The Tlic driver surged out of her car, reared up half her length before me. She was paler and smaller than T'Gatoi—probably born from the body of an animal. Tlic from Terran bodies were always larger as well as more numerous.

"Six young," I told her. "Maybe seven, all alive. At least one male."

"Lomas?" she said harshly. I liked her for the question and the concern in her voice when she asked it. The last coherent thing he had said was her name.

"He's alive," I said.

She surged away to the house without another word.

"She's been sick," my brother said, watching her go. "When I called, I could hear people telling her she wasn't well enough to go out even for this."

I said nothing. I had extended courtesy to the Tlic. Now I didn't want to talk to anyone. I hoped he would go in—out of curiosity if nothing else.

"Finally found out more than you wanted to know, eh?"

I looked at him.

"Don't give me one of *her* looks," he said. "You're not her. You're just her property."

One of her looks. Had I picked up even an ability to imitate her expressions?

"What'd you do, puke?" He sniffed the air. "So now you know what you're in for."

I walked away from him. He and I had been close when we were kids. He would let me follow him around when I was home, and sometimes T'Gatoi would let me bring him along when she took me into the city. But something had happened when he reached adolescence. I never knew what. He began keeping out of T'Gatoi's way. Then he began running away—until he realized there was no "away." Not in the Preserve. Certainly not outside. After that he concentrated on getting his share of every egg that came into the house and on looking out for me in a way that made me all but hate him—a way that clearly said, as long as I was all right, he was safe from the Tlic.

"How was it, really?" he demanded, following me.

"I killed an achti. The young ate it."

"You didn't run out of the house and puke because they ate an achti."

"I had . . . never seen a person cut open before." That was true, and enough for him to know. I couldn't talk about the other. Not with him.

"Oh," he said. He glanced at me as though he wanted to say more, but he kept quiet.

We walked, not really headed anywhere. Toward the back, toward the cages, toward the fields.

"Did he say anything?" Qui asked. "Lomas, I mean."

Who else would he mean? "He said 'T'Khotgif.' "

Qui shuddered. "If she had done that to me, she'd be the last person I'd call for."

"You'd call for her. Her sting would ease your pain without killing the grubs in you."

"You think I'd care if they died?"

No. Of course he wouldn't. Would I?

"Shit!" He drew a deep breath. "I've seen what they do. You think this thing with Lomas was bad? It was nothing."

I didn't argue. He didn't know what he was talking about.

"I saw them eat a man," he said.

I turned to face him. "You're lying!"

"*I saw them eat a man.*" He paused. "It was when I was little. I had been to the Hartmund house and I was on my way home. Halfway here, I saw a man and a Tlic and the man was N'Tlic. The ground was hilly. I was able to hide from them and watch. The Tlic wouldn't open the man because she had nothing to feed the grubs. The man couldn't go any further and there were no houses around. He was in so much pain, he told her to kill him. He begged her to kill him. Finally, she did. She cut his throat. One swipe of one claw. I saw the grubs eat their way out, then burrow in again, still eating."

His words made me see Lomas's flesh again, parasitized, crawling. "Why didn't you tell me that?" I whispered.

He looked startled as though he'd forgotten I was listening. "I don't know."

"You started to run away not long after that, didn't you?"

"Yeah. Stupid. Running inside the Preserve. Running in a cage."

I shook my head, said what I should have said to him long ago. "She wouldn't take you, Qui. You don't have to worry."

"She would . . . if anything happened to you."

"No. She'd take Xuan Hoa. Hoa . . . wants it." She wouldn't if she had stayed to watch Lomas.

"They don't take women," he said with contempt.

"They do sometimes." I glanced at him. "Actually, they prefer women. You should be around them when they talk among themselves. They say women have more body fat to protect the grubs. But they usually take men to leave the women free to bear their own young."

"To provide the next generation of host animals," he said, switching from contempt to bitterness.

"It's more than that!" I countered. Was it?

"If it were going to happen to me, I'd want to believe it was more, too."

"It *is* more!" I felt like a kid. Stupid argument.

"Did you think so while T'Gatoi was picking worms out of that guy's guts?"

"It's not supposed to happen that way."

"Sure it is. You weren't supposed to see it, that's all. And his Tlic was supposed to do it. She could sting him unconscious and the operation wouldn't have been as painful. But she'd still open him, pick out the grubs, and if she missed even one, it would poison him and eat him from the inside out."

There was actually a time when my mother told me to show respect for Qui because he was my older brother. I walked away, hating him. In his way, he was gloating. He was safe and I wasn't. I could have hit him, but I didn't think I would be able to stand it when he refused to hit back, when he looked at me with contempt and pity.

He wouldn't let me get away. Longer legged, he swung ahead of me and made me feel as though I were following him.

"I'm sorry," he said.

I strode on, sick and furious.

"Look, it probably won't be that bad with you. T'Gatoi likes you. She'll be careful."

I turned back toward the house, almost running from him.

"Has she done it to you yet?" he asked, keeping up easily. "I mean, you're about the right age for implantation. Has she—"

I hit him. I didn't know I was going to do it, but I think I meant to kill him. If he hadn't been bigger and stronger, I think I would have.

He tried to hold me off, but in the end, had to defend himself. He only hit me a couple of times. That was plenty. I don't remember going down, but when I came to, he was gone. It was worth the pain to be rid of him.

I got up and walked slowly toward the house. The back was dark. No one was in the kitchen. My mother and sisters were sleeping in their bedrooms—or pretending to.

Once I was in the kitchen, I could hear voices—Tlic and Terran from the next room. I couldn't make out what they were saying—didn't want to make it out.

I sat down at my mother's table, waiting for quiet. The table was smooth and worn, heavy and well crafted. My father had made it for her just before he died. I remembered hanging around underfoot when he built it. He didn't mind. Now I sat leaning on it, missing him. I could have talked to him. He had done it three times in his long life. Three clutches of eggs, three times being opened up and sewed up. How had he done it? How did anyone do it?

I got up, took the rifle from its hiding place, and sat down again with it. It needed cleaning, oiling.

All I did was load it.

"Gan?"

She made a lot of little clicking sounds when she walked on bare floor, each limb clicking in succession as it touched down. Waves of little clicks.

She came to the table, raised the front half of her body above it, and surged onto it. Sometimes she moved so smoothly she seemed to flow like water itself. She coiled herself into a small hill in the middle of the table and looked at me.

"That was bad," she said softly. "You should not have seen it. It need not be that way."

"I know."

"T'Khotgif—Ch'Khotgif now—she will die of her disease. She will not live to raise her children. But her sister will provide for them, and for Bram Lomas." Sterile sister. One fertile female in every lot. One to keep the family going. That sister owed Lomas more than she could ever repay.

"He'll live then?"

"Yes."

"I wonder if he would do it again."

"No one would ask him to do that again."

I looked into the yellow eyes, wondering how much I saw and understood there, and how much I only imagined. "No one ever asks us," I said. "You never asked me."

She moved her head slightly. "What's the matter with your face?"

"Nothing. Nothing important." Human eyes probably wouldn't have noticed the swelling in the darkness. The only light was from one of the moons, shining through a window across the room.

"Did you use the rifle to shoot the achti?"

"Yes."

"And do you mean to use it to shoot me?"

I stared at her, outlined in the moonlight—coiled, graceful body. "What does Terran blood taste like to you?"

She said nothing.

"What are you?" I whispered. "What are we to you?"

She lay still, rested her head on her topmost coil. "You know me as no other does," she said softly. "You must decide."

"That's what happened to my face," I told her.

"What?"

"Qui goaded me into deciding to do something. It didn't turn out very well." I moved the gun slightly, brought the barrel up diagonally under my own chin. "At least it was a decision I made."

"As this will be."

"Ask me, Gatoi."

"For my children's lives?"

She would say something like that. She knew how to manipulate people, Terran and Tlic. But not this time.

"I don't want to be a host animal," I said. "Not even yours."

It took her a long time to answer. "We use almost no host animals these days," she said. "You know that."

"You use us."

"We do. We wait long years for you and teach you and join our families to yours." She moved restlessly. "You know you aren't animals to us."

I stared at her, saying nothing.

"The animals we once used began killing most of our eggs after implantation long before your ancestors arrived," she said softly. "You know these things, Gan. Because your people arrived, we are relearning what it means to be a healthy, thriving people. And your ancestors, fleeing from their homeworld, from their own kind who would have killed or enslaved them—they survived because of us. We saw them as people and gave them the Preserve when they still tried to kill us as worms."

At the word "worms," I jumped. I couldn't help it, and she couldn't help noticing it.

"I see," she said quietly. "Would you really rather die than bear my young, Gan?"

I didn't answer.

"Shall I go to Xuan Hoa?"

"Yes!" Hoa wanted it. Let her have it. She hadn't had to watch Lomas. She'd be proud. . . . Not terrified.

T'Gatoi flowed off the table onto the floor, startling me almost too much.

"I'll sleep in Hoa's room tonight," she said. "And sometime tonight or in the morning, I'll tell her."

This was going too fast. My sister Hoa had had almost as much to do with raising me as my mother. I was still close to her—not like Qui. She could want T'Gatoi and still love me.

"Wait! Gatoi!"

She looked back, then raised nearly half her length off the floor and turned to face me. "These are adult things, Gan. This is my life, my family!"

"But she's . . . my sister."

"I have done what you demanded. I have asked you!"

"But—"

"It will be easier for Hoa. She has always expected to carry other lives inside her."

Human lives. Human young who should someday drink at her breasts, not at her veins.

I shook my head. "Don't do it to her, Gatoi." I was not Qui. It seemed I could become him, though, with no effort at all. I could make Xuan Hoa my shield. Would it be easier to know that red worms were growing in her flesh instead of mine?

"Don't do it to Hoa," I repeated.

She stared at me, utterly still.

I looked away, then back at her. "Do it to me."

I lowered the gun from my throat and she leaned forward to take it.

"No," I told her.

"It's the law," she said.

"Leave it for the family. One of them might use it to save my life someday."

She grasped the rifle barrel, but I wouldn't let go. I was pulled into a standing position over her.

"Leave it here!" I repeated. "If we're not your animals, if these are adult things, accept the risk. There is risk, Gatoi, in dealing with a partner."

It was clearly hard for her to let go of the rifle. A shudder went through her and she made a hissing sound of distress. It occurred to me that she was afraid. She was old enough to have seen what guns could do to people. Now her young and this gun would be together in the same house. She did not know about the other guns. In this dispute, they did not matter.

"I will implant the first egg tonight," she said as I put the gun away. "Do you hear, Gan?"

Why else had I been given a whole egg to eat while the rest of the family was left to share one? Why else had my mother kept looking at me as though I were going away from her, going where she could not follow? Did T'Gatoi imagine I hadn't known?

"I hear."

"Now!" I let her push me out of the kitchen, then walked ahead of her toward my bedroom. The sudden urgency in her voice sounded real. "You would have done it to Hoa tonight!" I accused.

"I must do it to someone tonight."

I stopped in spite of her urgency and stood in her way. "Don't you care who?"

She flowed around me and into my bedroom. I found her waiting on the couch we shared. There was nothing in Hoa's room that she could have used. She would have done it to Hoa on the floor. The thought of her doing it to Hoa at all disturbed me in a different way now, and I was suddenly angry.

Yet I undressed and lay down beside her. I knew what to do, what to expect. I had been told all my life. I felt the familiar sting, narcotic, mildly pleasant. Then the blind probing of her ovipositor. The puncture was painless, easy. So easy going in. She undulated slowly against me, her muscles forcing the egg from her body into mine. I held on to a pair of her limbs until I remembered Lomas holding her that way. Then I let go, moved inadvertently, and hurt her. She gave a low cry of pain and I expected to be caged at once within her limbs. When I wasn't, I held on to her again, feeling oddly ashamed.

"I'm sorry," I whispered.

She rubbed my shoulders with four of her limbs.

"Do you care?" I asked. "Do you care that it's me?"

She did not answer for some time. Finally, "You were the one making the choices tonight, Gan. I made mine long ago."

"Would you have gone to Hoa?"

"Yes. How could I put my children into the care of one who hates them?"

"It wasn't . . . hate."

"I know what it was."

"I was afraid."

Silence.

"I still am." I could admit it to her here, now.

"But you came to me . . . to save Hoa."

"Yes." I leaned my forehead against her. She was cool velvet, deceptively soft. "And to keep you for myself," I said. It was so. I didn't understand it, but it was so.

She made a soft hum of contentment. "I couldn't believe I had made such a mistake with you," she said. "I chose you. I believed you had grown to choose me."

"I had, but . . . "

"Lomas."

"Yes."

"I had never known a Terran to see a birth and take it well. Qui has seen one, hasn't he?"

"Yes."

"Terrans should be protected from seeing."

I didn't like the sound of that—and I doubted that it was possible. "Not protected," I said. "Shown. Shown when we're young kids, and shown more than once. Gatoi, no Terran ever sees a birth that goes right. All we see is N'Tlic—pain and terror and maybe death."

She looked down at me. "It is a private thing. It has always been a private thing."

Her tone kept me from insisting—that and the knowledge that if she changed her mind, I might be the first public example. But I had planted the thought in her mind. Chances were it would grow, and eventually she would experiment.

"You won't see it again," she said. "I don't want you thinking any more about shooting me."

The small amount of fluid that came into me with her egg relaxed me as completely as a sterile egg would have, so that I could remember the rifle in my hands and my feelings of fear and revulsion, anger and despair. I could remember the feelings without reviving them. I could talk about them.

"I wouldn't have shot you," I said. "Not you." She had been taken from my father's flesh when he was my age.

"You could have," she insisted.

"Not you." She stood between us and her own people, protecting, interweaving.

"Would you have destroyed yourself?"

I moved carefully, uncomfortable. "I could have done that. I nearly did. That's Qui's 'away.' I wonder if he knows."

"What?"

I did not answer.

"You will live now."

"Yes." *Take care of her,* my mother used to say. Yes.

"I'm healthy and young," she said. "I won't leave you as Lomas was left—alone, N'Tlic. I'll take care of you."

Afterword

It amazes me that some people have seen "Bloodchild" as a story of slavery. It isn't. It's a number of other things, though. On one level, it's a love story between two very different beings. On another, it's a coming-of-age story in which a boy must absorb disturbing information and use it to make a decision that will affect the rest of his life.

On a third level, "Bloodchild" is my pregnant man story. I've always wanted to explore what it might be like for a man to be put into that most unlikely of all positions. Could I write a story in which a man chose to become pregnant *not* through some sort of misplaced competitiveness to prove that a man could do anything a woman could do, not because he was forced to, not even out of curiosity? I wanted to see whether I could write a dramatic story of a man becoming pregnant as an act of love—choosing pregnancy in spite of as well as because of surrounding difficulties.

Also, "Bloodchild" was my effort to ease an old fear of mine. I was going to travel to the Peruvian Amazon to do research for my Xenogenesis books (*Dawn, Adulthood Rites,* and *Imago*), and I worried about my possible reactions to some of the insect life of the area. In particular, I worried about the botfly—an insect with, what seemed to me then, horror-movie habits. There was no shortage of botflies in the part of Peru that I intended to visit.

The botfly lays its eggs in wounds left by the bites of other insects. I found the idea of a maggot living and growing under my skin, eating my flesh as it grew, to be so intolerable, so terrifying that I didn't know how I could stand it if it happened to me. To make matters worse, all that I heard and read advised botfly victims not to try to get rid of their maggot passengers until they got back home to the United States and were able to go to a doctor—or until the fly finished the larval part of its growth cycle, crawled out of its host, and flew away.

The problem was to do what would seem to be the normal thing, to squeeze out the maggot and throw it away, was to invite infection. The maggot becomes literally attached to its host and leaves part of itself behind, broken off, if it's squeezed or cut out. Of course, the part left behind dies and rots, causing infection. Lovely.

When I have to deal with something that disturbs me as much as the botfly did, I write about it. I sort out my problems by writing about them. In a high school classroom on November 22, 1963, I remember grabbing a notebook and beginning to write my response to news of John Kennedy's assassination. Whether I write journal pages, an essay, a short story, or weave my problems into a novel, I find the writing helps me get through the trouble and get on with my life. Writing "Bloodchild" didn't make me like botflies, but for a while, it made them seem more interesting than horrifying.

There's one more thing I tried to do in "Bloodchild." I tried to write a story about paying the rent—a story about an isolated colony of human beings on an inhabited, extrasolar world. At best, they would be a lifetime away from reinforcements. It wouldn't be the British Empire in space, and it wouldn't be *Star Trek*. Sooner or later, the humans would have to make some kind of accommodation with their um . . . their hosts. Chances are this would be an unusual accommodation. Who knows what we humans have that others might be willing to take in trade for a livable space on a world not our own?

The Evening and the Morning and the Night

When I was fifteen and trying to show my independence by getting careless with my diet, my parents took me to a Duryea-Gode disease ward. They wanted me to see, they said, where I was headed if I wasn't careful. In fact, it was where I was headed no matter what. It was only a matter of when: now or later. My parents were putting in their vote for later.

I won't describe the ward. It's enough to say that when they brought me home, I cut my wrists. I did a thorough job of it, old Roman style in a bathtub of warm water. Almost made it. My father dislocated his shoulder breaking down the bathroom door. He and I never forgave each other for that day.

The disease got him almost three years later—just before I went off to college. It was sudden. It doesn't happen that way often. Most people notice themselves beginning to drift—or their relatives notice—and they make arrangements with their chosen institution. People who are noticed and who resist going in can be locked up for a week's observation. I don't doubt that that observation period breaks up a few families. Sending someone away for what turns out to be a false alarm. . . . Well, it isn't the sort of thing the victim is likely to forgive or forget. On the other hand, not sending someone away in time—missing the signs or having a person go off suddenly without signs—is inevitably dangerous for the victim. I've never heard of it going as badly, though, as it did in my family. People normally injure only themselves when their time comes—unless someone is stupid enough to try to handle them without the necessary drugs or restraints.

My father had killed my mother, then killed himself. I wasn't home when it happened. I had stayed at school later than usual, rehearsing graduation exercises. By the time I got home, there were cops everywhere. There was an ambulance, and two attendants were wheeling someone out on a stretcher—someone covered. More than covered. Almost . . . bagged.

The cops wouldn't let me in. I didn't find out until later exactly what had happened. I wish I'd never found out. Dad had killed Mom, then skinned her completely. At least that's how I hope it happened. I mean I hope he killed her first. He broke some of her ribs, damaged her heart. Digging.

Then he began tearing at himself, through skin and bone, digging. He had managed to reach his own heart before he died. It was an especially bad example of the kind of thing that makes people afraid of us. It gets some of us into trouble for picking at a pimple or even for daydreaming. It has inspired restrictive laws, created problems with jobs, housing, schools. . . . The Duryea-Gode Disease Foundation has spent millions telling the world that people like my father don't exist.

A long time later, when I had gotten myself together as best I could, I went to college—to the University of Southern California—on a Dilg scholarship. Dilg is the retreat you try to send your out-of-control DGD relatives to. It's run by controlled DGDs like me, like my parents while they lived. God knows how any controlled DGD stands it. Anyway, the place has a waiting list miles long. My parents put me on it after my suicide attempt, but chances were, I'd be dead by the time my name came up.

I can't say why I went to college—except that I had been going to school all my life and didn't know what else to do. I didn't go with any particular hope. Hell, I knew what I was in for eventually. I was just marking time. Whatever I did was just marking time. If people were willing to pay me to go to school and mark time, why not do it?

The weird part was, I worked hard, got top grades. If you work hard enough at something that doesn't matter, you can forget for a while about the things that do.

Sometimes I thought about trying suicide again. How was it I'd had the courage when I was fifteen but didn't have it now? Two DGD parents—both religious, both as opposed to abortion as they were to suicide. So they had trusted God and the promises of modern medicine and had a child. But how could I look at what had happened to them and trust anything?

I majored in biology. Non-DGDs say something about our disease makes us good at the sciences—genetics, molecular biology, biochemistry. . . . That something was terror. Terror and a kind of driving hopelessness. Some of us went bad and became destructive before we had to—yes, we did produce more than our share of criminals. And some of us went good—spectacularly—and made scientific and medical history. These last kept the doors at least partly open for the rest of us. They made discoveries in genetics, found cures for a couple of rare diseases, made advances against other diseases that weren't so rare—including, ironically, some forms of cancer. But they'd found nothing to help themselves. There had been nothing since the latest improvements in the diet, and those came just before I was born. They, like the original diet, gave more DGDs the courage to have children. They were supposed to do for DGDs what insulin had done for diabetics—give us a normal or nearly normal life span. Maybe they had worked for someone somewhere. They hadn't worked for anyone I knew.

Biology school was a pain in the usual ways. I didn't eat in public anymore, didn't like the way people stared at my biscuits—cleverly dubbed "dog biscuits" in every school I'd ever attended. You'd think university students would be more creative. I didn't like the way people edged away from me when they caught sight of my emblem. I'd begun wearing it on a chain around my neck and putting it down inside my blouse, but people managed to notice it anyway. People who don't eat in public, who drink nothing more interesting than water, who smoke nothing at all—people like that are suspicious. Or rather, they make others suspicious. Sooner or later, one of those others, finding my fingers and wrists bare, would fake an interest in my chain. That would be that. I couldn't hide the emblem in my purse. If anything happened to me, medical people had to see it in time to avoid giving me the medications they might use on a normal person. It isn't just ordinary food we have to avoid, but about a quarter of a *Physicians' Desk Reference* of widely used drugs. Every now and then there are news stories about people who stopped carrying their emblems—probably trying to pass as normal. Then they have an accident. By the time anyone realizes there is anything wrong, it's too late. So I wore my emblem. And one way or another, people got a look at it or got the word from someone who had. "She *is*!" Yeah.

At the beginning of my third year, four other DGDs and I decided to rent a house together. We'd all had enough of being lepers twenty-four hours a day. There was an English major. He wanted to be a writer and tell our story from the inside—which had only been done thirty or forty times before. There was a special-education major who hoped the handicapped would accept her more readily than the able-bodied, a premed who planned to go into research, and a chemistry major who didn't really know what she wanted to do.

Two men and three women. All we had in common was our disease, plus a weird combination of stubborn intensity about whatever we happened to be doing and hopeless cynicism about everything else. Healthy people say no one can concentrate like a DGD. Healthy people have all the time in the world for stupid generalizations and short attention spans.

We did our work, came up for air now and then, ate our biscuits, and attended classes. Our only problem was housecleaning. We worked out a schedule of who would clean what when, who would deal with the yard, whatever. We all agreed on it; then, except for me, everyone seemed to forget about it. I found myself going around reminding people to vacuum, clean the bathroom, mow the lawn. . . . I figured they'd all hate me in no time, but I wasn't going to be their maid, and I wasn't going to live in filth. Nobody complained. Nobody even seemed annoyed. They just came up out of their academic daze, cleaned, mopped, mowed, and went back to it. I got into the habit of running around in the evening reminding people. It didn't bother me if it didn't bother them.

"How'd you get to be housemother?" a visiting DGD asked.

I shrugged. "Who cares? The house works." It did. It worked so well that this new guy wanted to move in. He was a friend of one of the others, and another premed. Not bad looking.

"So do I get in or don't I?" he asked.

"As far as I'm concerned, you do," I said. I did what his friend should have done—introduced him around, then, after he left, talked to the others to make sure nobody had any real objections. He seemed to fit right in. He forgot to clean the toilet or mow the lawn, just like the others. His name was Alan Chi. I thought Chi was a Chinese name, and I wondered. But he told me his father was Nigerian and that in Ibo the word meant a kind of guardian angel or personal God. He said his own personal God hadn't been looking out for him very well to let him be born to two DGD parents. Him too.

I don't think it was much more than that similarity that drew us together at first. Sure, I liked the way he looked, but I was used to liking someone's looks and having him run like hell when he found out what I was. It took me a while to get used to the fact that Alan wasn't going anywhere.

I told him about my visit to the DGD ward when I was fifteen—and my suicide attempt afterward. I had never told anyone else. I was surprised at how relieved it made me feel to tell him. And somehow his reaction didn't surprise me.

"Why didn't you try again?" he asked. We were alone in the living room.

"At first, because of my parents," I said. "My father in particular. I couldn't do that to him again."

"And after him?"

"Fear. Inertia."

He nodded. "When I do it, there'll be no half measures. No being rescued, no waking up in a hospital later."

"You mean to do it?"

"The day I realize I've started to drift. Thank God we get some warning."

"Not necessarily."

"Yes, we do. I've done a lot of reading. Even talked to a couple of doctors. Don't believe the rumors non-DGDs invent."

I looked away, stared into the scarred, empty fireplace. I told him exactly how my father had died—something else I'd never voluntarily told anyone.

He sighed. "Jesus!"

We looked at each other.

"What are you going to do?" he asked.

"I don't know."

He extended a dark, square hand, and I took it and moved closer to him. He was a dark, square man—my height, half again my weight, and none of it fat. He was so bitter sometimes, he scared me.

"My mother started to drift when I was three," he said. "My father only lasted a few months longer. I heard he died a couple of years after he went into the hospital. If the two of them had had any sense, they would have had me aborted the minute my mother realized she was pregnant. But she wanted a kid no matter what. And she was Catholic." He shook his head. "Hell, they should pass a law to sterilize the lot of us."

"They?" I said.

"You want kids?"

"No, but—"

"More like us to wind up chewing their fingers off in some DGD ward."

"I don't want kids, but I don't want someone else telling me I can't have any."

He stared at me until I began to feel stupid and defensive. I moved away from him.

"Do you want someone else telling you what to do with your body?" I asked.

"No need," he said. "I had that taken care of as soon as I was old enough."

This left me staring. I'd thought about sterilization. What DGD hasn't? But I didn't know anyone else our age who had actually gone through with it. That would be like killing part of yourself—even though it wasn't a part you intended to use. Killing part of yourself when so much of you was already dead.

"The damned disease could be wiped out in one generation," he said, "but people are still animals when it comes to breeding. Still following mindless urges, like dogs and cats."

My impulse was to get up and go away, leave him to wallow in his bitterness and depression alone. But I stayed. He seemed to want to live even less than I did. I wondered how he'd made it this far.

"Are you looking forward to doing research?" I probed. "Do you believe you'll be able to—"

"No."

I blinked. The word was as cold and dead a sound as I'd ever heard.

"I don't believe in anything," he said.

I took him to bed. He was the only other double DGD I had ever met, and if nobody did anything for him, he wouldn't last much longer. I couldn't just let him slip away. For a while, maybe we could be each other's reasons for staying alive.

He was a good student—for the same reason I was. And he seemed to shed some of his bitterness as time passed. Being around him helped me understand why, against all sanity, two DGDs would lock in on each other and start talking about marriage. Who else would have us?

We probably wouldn't last very long, anyway. These days, most DGDs make it to forty, at least. But then, most of them don't have two DGD parents. As bright as Alan was, he might not get into medical school because of his double inheritance. No one would tell him his bad genes were keeping him out, of course, but we both knew what his chances were. Better to train doctors who were likely to live long enough to put their training to use.

Alan's mother had been sent to Dilg. He hadn't seen her or been able to get any information about her from his grandparents while he was at home. By the time he left for college, he'd stopped asking questions. Maybe it was hearing about my parents that made him start again. I was with him when he called Dilg. Until that moment, he hadn't even known whether his mother was still alive. Surprisingly, she was.

"Dilg must be good," I said when he hung up. "People don't usually . . . I mean . . . "

"Yeah, I know," he said. "People don't usually live long once they're out of control. Dilg is different." We had gone to my room, where he turned a chair backward and sat down. "Dilg is what the others ought to be, if you can believe the literature."

"Dilg is a giant DGD ward," I said. "It's richer—probably better at sucking in the donations—and it's run by people who can expect to become patients eventually. Apart from that, what's different?"

"I've read about it," he said. "So should you. They've got some new treatment. They don't just shut people away to die the way the others do."

"What else is there to do with them? With us."

"I don't know. It sounded like they have some kind of . . . sheltered workshop. They've got patients doing things."

"A new drug to control the self-destructiveness?"

"I don't think so. We would have heard about that."

"What else could it be?"

"I'm going up to find out. Will you come with me?"

"You're going up to see your mother."

He took a ragged breath. "Yeah. Will you come with me?"

I went to one of my windows and stared out at the weeds. We let them thrive in the backyard. In the front we mowed them, along with the few patches of grass.

"I told you my DGD-ward experience."

"You're not fifteen now. And Dilg isn't some zoo of a ward."

"It's got to be, no matter what they tell the public. And I'm not sure I can stand it."

He got up, came to stand next to me. "Will you try?"

I didn't say anything. I focused on our reflections in the window glass—the two of us together. It looked right, felt right. He put his arm around me, and I leaned back against him. Our being together had been as good for me as it seemed to have been for him. It had given me something to go on besides inertia and fear. I knew I would go with him. It felt like the right thing to do.

"I can't say how I'll act when we get there," I said.

"I can't say how I'll act, either," he admitted. "Especially . . . when I see her."

He made the appointment for the next Saturday afternoon. You make appointments to go to Dilg unless you're a government inspector of some kind. That is the custom, and Dilg gets away with it.

We left L.A. in the rain early Saturday morning. Rain followed us off and on up the coast as far as Santa Barbara. Dilg was hidden away in the hills not far from San Jose. We could have reached it faster by driving up I-5, but neither of us were in the mood for all that bleakness. As it was, we arrived at one P.M. to be met by two armed gate guards. One of these phoned the main building and verified our appointment. Then the other took the wheel from Alan.

"Sorry," he said. "But no one is permitted inside without an escort. We'll meet your guide at the garage."

None of this surprised me. Dilg is a place where not only the patients but much of the staff has DGD. A maximum security prison wouldn't have been as potentially dangerous. On the other hand, I'd never heard of anyone getting chewed up here. Hospitals and rest homes had accidents. Dilg didn't.

It was beautiful—an old estate. One that didn't make sense in these days of high taxes. It had been owned by the Dilg family. Oil, chemicals, pharmaceuticals. Ironically, they had even owned part of the late, unlamented Hedeon Laboratories. They'd had a briefly profitable interest in Hedeonco: the magic bullet, the cure for a large percentage of the world's cancer and a number of serious viral diseases—and the cause of Duryea-Gode disease. If one of your parents was treated with Hedeonco and you were conceived after the treatments, you had DGD. If you had kids, you passed it on to them. Not everyone was equally affected. They didn't all commit suicide or murder, but they all mutilated themselves to some degree if they could. And they all drifted—went off into a world of their own and stopped responding to their surroundings.

Anyway, the only Dilg son of his generation had had his life saved by Hedeonco. Then he had watched four of his children die before Doctors Kenneth Duryea and Jan Gode came up with a decent understanding of the problem and a partial solution: the diet. They gave Richard Dilg a way of keeping his next two children alive. He gave the big, cumbersome estate over to the care of DGD patients.

So the main building was an elaborate old mansion. There were other, newer buildings, more like guest houses than institutional buildings. And there were wooded hills all around. Nice country. Green. The ocean wasn't far away. There was an old garage and a small parking lot. Waiting in the lot was a tall, old woman. Our guard pulled up near her, let us out, then parked the car in the half-empty garage.

"Hello," the woman said, extending her hand. "I'm Beatrice Alcantara." The hand was cool and dry and startlingly strong. I thought the woman was DGD, but her age threw me. She appeared to be about sixty, and I had never seen a DGD that old. I wasn't sure why I thought she was DGD. If she was, she must have been an experimental model—one of the first to survive.

"Is it Doctor or Ms.?" Alan asked.

"It's Beatrice," she said. "I am a doctor, but we don't use titles much here."

I glanced at Alan, was surprised to see him smiling at her. He tended to go a long time between smiles. I looked at Beatrice and couldn't see anything to smile about. As we introduced ourselves, I realized I didn't like her. I couldn't see any reason for that either, but my feelings were my feelings. I didn't like her.

"I assume neither of you have been here before," she said, smiling down at us. She was at least six feet tall, and straight.

We shook our heads. "Let's go in the front way, then. I want to prepare you for what we do here. I don't want you to believe you've come to a hospital."

I frowned at her, wondering what else there was to believe. Dilg was called a retreat, but what difference did names make?

The house close up looked like one of the old-style public buildings—massive, baroque front with a single domed tower reaching three stories above the three-story house. Wings of the house stretched for some distance to the right and left of the tower, then cornered and stretched back twice as far. The front doors were huge—one set of wrought iron and one of heavy wood. Neither appeared to be locked.

Beatrice pulled open the iron door, pushed the wooden one, and gestured us in.

Inside, the house was an art museum—huge, high ceilinged, tile floored. There were marble columns and niches in which sculptures stood or paintings hung. There were other sculptures displayed around the rooms. At one end of the rooms there was a broad staircase leading up to a gallery that went around the rooms. There more art was displayed. "All this was made here," Beatrice said. "Some of it is even sold from here. Most goes to galleries in the Bay Area or down around L.A. Our only problem is turning out too much of it."

"You mean the patients do this?" I asked.

The old woman nodded. "This and much more. Our people work instead of tearing at themselves or staring into space. One of them invented the p.v. locks that protect this place. Though I almost wish he hadn't. It's gotten us more government attention than we like."

"What kind of locks?" I asked.

"Sorry. Palmprint-voiceprint. The first and the best. We have the patent." She looked at Alan. "Would you like to see what your mother does?"

"Wait a minute," he said. "You're telling us out-of-control DGDs create art and invent things?"

"And that lock," I said. "I've never heard of anything like that. I didn't even see a lock."

"The lock is new," she said. "There have been a few news stories about it. It's not the kind of thing most people would buy for their homes. Too expensive. So it's of limited interest. People tend to look at what's done at Dilg in the way they look at the efforts of idiots savants. Interesting, incomprehensible, but not really important. Those likely to be interested in the lock and able to afford it know about it." She took a deep breath, faced Alan again. "Oh, yes, DGDs create things. At least they do here."

"Out-of-control DGDs."

"Yes."

"I expected to find them weaving baskets or something—at best. I know what DGD wards are like."

"So do I," she said. "I know what they're like in hospitals, and I know what it's like here." She waved a hand toward an abstract painting that looked like a photo I had once seen of the Orion Nebula. Darkness broken by a great cloud of light and color. "Here we can help them channel their energies. They can create something beautiful, useful, even something worthless. But they create. They don't destroy."

"Why?" Alan demanded. "It can't be some drug. We would have heard."

"It's not a drug."

"Then what is it? Why haven't other hospitals—?"

"Alan," she said. "Wait."

He stood frowning at her.

"Do you want to see your mother?"

"Of course I want to see her!"

"Good. Come with me. Things will sort themselves out."

She led us to a corridor past offices where people talked to one another, waved to Beatrice, worked with computers. . . . They could have been anywhere. I wondered how many of them were controlled DGDs. I also wondered what kind of game the old woman was playing with her secrets. We passed through rooms so beautiful and perfectly kept it was obvious they were rarely used. Then at a broad, heavy door, she stopped us.

"Look at anything you like as we go on," she said. "But don't touch anything or anyone. And remember that some of the people you'll see injured themselves before they came to us. They still bear the scars of those injuries. Some of those scars may be difficult to look at, but you'll be in no danger. Keep that in mind. No one here will harm you." She pushed the door open and gestured us in.

Scars didn't bother me much. Disability didn't bother me. It was the act of self-mutilation that scared me. It was someone attacking her own arm as though it were a wild animal. It was someone who had torn at himself and been restrained or drugged off and on for so long that he barely had a recognizable human feature left, but he was still trying with what he did have to dig into his own flesh. Those are a couple of the things I saw at the DGD ward when I was fifteen. Even then I could have stood it better if I hadn't felt I was looking into a kind of temporal mirror.

I wasn't aware of walking through that doorway. I wouldn't have thought I could do it. The old woman said something, though, and I found myself on the other side of the door with the door closing behind me. I turned to stare at her.

She put her hand on my arm. "It's all right," she said quietly. "That door looks like a wall to a great many people."

I backed away from her, out of her reach, repelled by her touch. Shaking hands had been enough, for God's sake.

Something in her seemed to come to attention as she watched me. It made her even straighter. Deliberately, but for no apparent reason, she stepped toward Alan, touched him the way people do sometimes when they brush past—a kind of tactile "Excuse me." In that wide, empty corridor, it was totally unnecessary. For some reason, she wanted to touch him and wanted me to see. What did she think she was doing? Flirting at her age? I glared at her, found myself suppressing an irrational urge to shove her away from him. The violence of the urge amazed me.

Beatrice smiled and turned away. "This way," she said. Alan put his arm around me and tried to lead me after her.

"Wait a minute," I said, not moving.

Beatrice glanced around.

"What just happened?" I asked. I was ready for her to lie—to say nothing happened, pretend not to know what I was talking about.

"Are you planning to study medicine?" she asked.

"What? What does that have to do—?"

"Study medicine. You may be able to do a great deal of good." She strode away, taking long steps so that we had to hurry to keep up. She led us through a room in which some people worked at computer terminals and others with pencils and paper. It would have been an ordinary scene except that some people had half their faces ruined or had only one hand or leg or had other obvious scars. But they were all in control now. They were working. They were intent but not intent on self-destruction. Not one was digging into or tearing away flesh. When we had passed through this room and into a small, ornate sitting room, Alan grasped Beatrice's arm.

"What is it?" he demanded. "What do you do for them?"

She patted his hand, setting my teeth on edge. "I will tell you," she said. "I want you to know. But I want you to see your mother first." To my surprise, he nodded, let it go at that.

"Sit a moment," she said to us.

We sat in comfortable, matching upholstered chairs—Alan looking reasonably relaxed. What was it about the old lady that relaxed him but put me on edge? Maybe she reminded him of his grandmother or something. She didn't remind me of anyone. And what was that nonsense about studying medicine?

"I wanted you to pass through at least one workroom before we talked about your mother—and about the two of you." She turned to face me. "You've had a bad experience at a hospital or a rest home?"

I looked away from her, not wanting to think about it. Hadn't the people in that mock office been enough of a reminder? Horror film office. Nightmare office.

"It's all right," she said. "You don't have to go into detail. Just outline it for me."

I obeyed slowly, against my will, all the while wondering why I was doing it.

She nodded, unsurprised. "Harsh, loving people, your parents. Are they alive?"

"No."

"Were they both DGD?"

"Yes, but . . . yes."

"Of course, aside from the obvious ugliness of your hospital experience and its implications for the future, what impressed you about the people in the ward?"

I didn't know what to answer. What did she want? Why did she want anything from me? She should have been concerned with Alan and his mother.

"Did you see people unrestrained?"

"Yes," I whispered. "One woman. I don't know how it happened that she was free. She ran up to us and slammed into my father without moving him. He was a big man. She bounced off, fell, and . . . began tearing at herself. She bit her own arm and . . . swallowed the flesh she'd bitten away. She tore at the wound she'd made with the nails of her other hand. She . . . I screamed at her to stop." I hugged myself, remembering the young woman, bloody, cannibalizing herself as she lay at our feet, digging into her own flesh. Digging. "They try so hard, fight so hard to get out."

"Out of what?" Alan demanded.

I looked at him, hardly seeing him.

"Lynn," he said gently. "Out of what?"

I shook my head. "Their restraints, their disease, the ward, their bodies . . ."

He glanced at Beatrice, then spoke to me again. "Did the girl talk?"

"No. She screamed."

He turned away from me uncomfortably. "Is this important?" he asked Beatrice.

"Very," she said.

"Well . . . can we talk about it after I see my mother?"

"Then and now." She spoke to me. "Did the girl stop what she was doing when you told her to?"

"The nurses had her a moment later. It didn't matter."

"It mattered. Did she stop?"

"Yes."

"According to the literature, they rarely respond to anyone," Alan said.

"True." Beatrice gave him a sad smile. "Your mother will probably respond to you, though."

"Is she? . . . " He glanced back at the nightmare office. "Is she as controlled as those people?"

"Yes, though she hasn't always been. Your mother works with clay now. She loves shapes and textures and—"

"She's blind," Alan said, voicing the suspicion as though it were fact. Beatrice's words had sent my thoughts in the same direction. Beatrice hesitated. "Yes," she said finally. "And for . . . the usual reason. I had intended to prepare you slowly."

"I've done a lot of reading."

I hadn't done much reading, but I knew what the usual reason was. The woman had gouged, ripped, or otherwise destroyed her eyes. She would be badly scarred. I got up, went over to sit on the arm of Alan's chair. I rested my hand on his shoulder, and he reached up and held it there.

"Can we see her now?" he asked.

Beatrice got up. "This way," she said.

We passed through more workrooms. People painted; assembled machinery; sculpted in wood, stone; even composed and played music. Almost no one noticed us. The patients were true to their disease in that respect. They weren't ignoring us. They clearly didn't know we existed. Only the few controlled-DGD guards gave themselves away by waving or speaking to Beatrice. I watched a woman work quickly, knowledgeably, with a power saw. She obviously understood the perimeters of her body, was not so dissociated as to perceive herself as trapped in something she needed to dig her way out of. What had Dilg done for these people that other hospitals did not do? And how could Dilg withhold its treatment from the others?

"Over there we make our own diet foods," Beatrice said, pointing through a window toward one of the guest houses. "We permit more variety and make fewer mistakes than the commercial preparers. No ordinary person can concentrate on work the way our people can."

I turned to face her. "What are you saying? That the bigots are right? That we have some special gift?"

"Yes," she said. "It's hardly a bad characteristic, is it?"

"It's what people say whenever one of us does well at something. It's their way of denying us credit for our work."

"Yes. But people occasionally come to the right conclusions for the wrong reasons." I shrugged, not interested in arguing with her about it.

"Alan?" she said. He looked at her.

"Your mother is in the next room."

He swallowed, nodded. We both followed her into the room.

Naomi Chi was a small woman, hair still dark, fingers long and thin, graceful as they shaped the clay. Her face was a ruin. Not only her eyes but most of her nose and one ear were gone. What was left was badly scarred. "Her parents were poor," Beatrice said. "I don't know how much they told you, Alan, but they went through all the money they had, trying to keep her at a decent place. Her mother felt so guilty, you know. She was the one who had cancer and took the drug. . . . Eventually, they had to put Naomi in one of those state-approved, custodial-care places. You know the kind. For a while, it was all the government would pay for. Places like that . . . well, sometimes if patients were really troublesome—especially the ones who kept breaking free—they'd put them in a bare room and let them finish themselves. The only things those places took good care of were the maggots, the cockroaches, and the rats."

I shuddered. "I've heard there are still places like that."

"There are," Beatrice said, "kept open by greed and indifference." She looked at Alan. "Your mother survived for three months in one of those places. I took her from it myself. Later I was instrumental in having that particular place closed."

"You took her?" I asked.

"Dilg didn't exist then, but I was working with a group of controlled DGDs in L.A. Naomi's parents heard about us and asked us to take her. A lot of people didn't trust us then. Only a few of us were medically trained. All of us were young, idealistic, and ignorant. We began in an old frame house with a leaky roof. Naomi's parents were grabbing at straws. So were we. And by pure luck, we grabbed a good one. We were able to prove ourselves to the Dilg family and take over these quarters."

"Prove what?" I asked.

She turned to look at Alan and his mother. Alan was staring at Naomi's ruined face, at the ropy, discolored scar tissue. Naomi was shaping the image of an old woman and two children. The gaunt, lined face of the old woman was remarkably vivid—detailed in a way that seemed impossible for a blind sculptress.

Naomi seemed unaware of us. Her total attention remained on her work. Alan forgot about what Beatrice had told us and reached out to touch the scarred face.

Beatrice let it happen. Naomi did not seem to notice. "If I get her attention for you," Beatrice said, "we'll be breaking her routine. We'll have to stay with her until she gets back into it without hurting herself. About half an hour."

"You can get her attention?" he asked.

"Yes."

"Can she? . . . " Alan swallowed. "I've never heard of anything like this. Can she talk?"

"Yes. She may not choose to, though. And if she does, she'll do it very slowly."

"Do it. Get her attention."

"She'll want to touch you."

"That's all right. Do it."

Beatrice took Naomi's hands and held them still, away from the wet clay. For several seconds Naomi tugged at her captive hands, as though unable to understand why they did not move as she wished.

Beatrice stepped closer and spoke quietly. "Stop, Naomi." And Naomi was still, blind face turned toward Beatrice in an attitude of attentive waiting. Totally focused waiting.

"Company, Naomi."

After a few seconds, Naomi made a wordless sound.

Beatrice gestured Alan to her side, gave Naomi one of his hands. It didn't bother me this time when she touched him. I was too interested in what was happening. Naomi examined Alan's hand minutely, then followed the arm up to the shoulder, the neck, the face. Holding his face between her hands, she made a sound. It may have been a word, but I couldn't understand it. All I could think of was the danger of those hands. I thought of my father's hands.

"His name is Alan Chi, Naomi. He's your son." Several seconds passed.

"Son?" she said. This time the word was quite distinct, though her lips had split in many places and had healed badly. "Son?" she repeated anxiously. "Here?"

"He's all right, Naomi. He's come to visit."

"Mother?" he said.

She reexamined his face. He had been three when she started to drift. It didn't seem possible that she could find anything in his face that she would remember. I wondered whether she remembered she had a son.

"Alan?" she said. She found his tears and paused at them. She touched her own face where there should have been an eye, then she reached back toward his eyes. An instant before I would have grabbed her hand, Beatrice did it.

"No!" Beatrice said firmly.

The hand fell limply to Naomi's side. Her face turned toward Beatrice like an antique weather vane swinging around. Beatrice stroked her hair, and Naomi said something I almost understood. Beatrice looked at Alan, who was frowning and wiping away tears.

"Hug your son," Beatrice said softly.

Naomi turned, groping, and Alan seized her in a tight, long hug. Her arms went around him slowly. She spoke words blurred by her ruined mouth but just understandable.

"Parents?" she said. "Did my parents . . . care for you?" Alan looked at her, clearly not understanding.

"She wants to know whether her parents took care of you," I said.

He glanced at me doubtfully, then looked at Beatrice.

"Yes," Beatrice said. "She just wants to know that they cared for you."

"They did," he said. "They kept their promise to you, Mother."

Several seconds passed. Naomi made sounds that even Alan took to be weeping, and he tried to comfort her.

"Who else is here?" she said finally.

This time Alan looked at me. I repeated what she had said.

"Her name is Lynn Mortimer," he said. "I'm . . . " He paused awkwardly. "She and I are going to be married."

After a time, she moved back from him and said my name. My first impulse was to go to her. I wasn't afraid or repelled by her now, but for no reason I could explain, I looked at Beatrice.

"Go," she said. "But you and I will have to talk later."

I went to Naomi, took her hand.

"Bea?" she said.

"I'm Lynn," I said softly.

She drew a quick breath. "No," she said. "No, you're . . ."

"I'm Lynn. Do you want Bea? She's here."

She said nothing. She put her hand to my face, explored it slowly. I let her do it, confident that I could stop her if she turned violent. But first one hand, then both, went over me very gently.

"You'll marry my son?" she said finally.

"Yes."

"Good. You'll keep him safe."

As much as possible, we'll keep each other safe. "Yes," I said.

"Good. No one will close him away from himself. No one will tie him or cage him." Her hand wandered to her own face again, nails biting in slightly.

"No," I said softly, catching the hand. "I want you to be safe, too."

The mouth moved. I think it smiled. "Son?" she said.

He understood her, took her hand.

"Clay," she said. Lynn and Alan in clay. "Bea?"

Of course," Beatrice said. "Do you have an impression?"

"No!" It was the fastest that Naomi had answered anything. Then, almost childlike, she whispered. "Yes."

Beatrice laughed. "Touch them again if you like, Naomi. They don't mind."

We didn't. Alan closed his eyes, trusting her gentleness in a way I could not. I had no trouble accepting her touch, even so near my eyes, but I did not delude myself about her. Her gentleness could turn in an instant. Naomi's fingers twitched near Alan's eyes, and I spoke up at once, out of fear for him.

"Just touch him, Naomi. Only touch."

She froze, made an interrogative sound.

"She's all right," Alan said.

"I know," I said, not believing it. He would be all right, though, as long as someone watched her very carefully, nipped any dangerous impulses in the bud.

"Son!" she said, happily possessive. When she let him go, she demanded clay, wouldn't touch her old-woman sculpture again. Beatrice got new clay for her, leaving us to soothe her and ease her impatience. Alan began to recognize signs of impending destructive behavior. Twice he caught her hands and said no. She struggled against him until I spoke to her. As

Beatrice returned, it happened again, and Beatrice said, "No, Naomi." Obediently Naomi let her hands fall to her sides.

"What is it?" Alan demanded later when we had left Naomi safely, totally focused on her new work—clay sculptures of us. "Does she only listen to women or something?"

Beatrice took us back to the sitting room, sat us both down, but did not sit down herself. She went to a window and stared out. "Naomi only obeys certain women," she said. "And she's sometimes slow to obey. She's worse than most—probably because of the damage she managed to do to herself before I got her." Beatrice faced us, stood biting her lip and frowning. "I haven't had to give this particular speech for a while," she said. "Most DGDs have the sense not to marry each other and produce children. I hope you two aren't planning to have any—in spite of our need." She took a deep breath. "It's a pheromone. A scent. And it's sex-linked. Men who inherit the disease from their fathers have no trace of the scent. They also tend to have an easier time with the disease. But they're useless to use as staff here. Men who inherit from their mothers have as much of the scent as men get. They can be useful here because the DGDs can at least be made to notice them. The same for women who inherit from their mothers but not their fathers. It's only when two irresponsible DGDs get together and produce girl children like me or Lynn that you get someone who can really do some good in a place like this." She looked at me. "We are very rare commodities, you and I. When you finish school you'll have a very well-paying job waiting for you."

"Here?" I asked.

"For training, perhaps. Beyond that, I don't know. You'll probably help start a retreat in some other part of the country.

Others are badly needed." She smiled humorlessly. "People like us don't get along well together. You must realize that I don't like you any more than you like me."

I swallowed, saw her through a kind of haze for a moment. Hated her mindlessly—just for a moment.

"Sit back," she said. "Relax your body. It helps."

I obeyed, not really wanting to obey her but unable to think of anything else to do. Unable to think at all. "We seem," she said, "to be very territorial. Dilg is a haven for me when I'm the only one of my kind here. When I'm not, it's a prison."

"All it looks like to me is an unbelievable amount of work," Alan said.

She nodded. "Almost too much." She smiled to herself. "I was one of the first double DGDs to be born. When I was old enough to understand, I thought I didn't have much time. First I tried to kill myself. Failing that, I tried to cram all the living I could into the small amount of time I assumed I had. When I got into this project, I worked as hard as I could to get it into shape before I started to drift. By now I wouldn't know what to do with myself if I weren't working."

"Why haven't you . . . drifted?" I asked.

"I don't know. There aren't enough of our kind to know what's normal for us."

"Drifting is normal for every DGD sooner or later."

"Later, then."

"Why hasn't the scent been synthesized?" Alan asked. "Why are there still concentration-camp rest homes and hospital wards?"

"There have been people trying to synthesize it since I proved what I could do with it. No one has succeeded so far.

All we've been able to do is keep our eyes open for people like Lynn." She looked at me. "Dilg scholarship, right?"

"Yeah. Offered out of the blue."

"My people do a good job keeping track. You would have been contacted just before you graduated or if you dropped out."

"Is it possible," Alan said, staring at me, "that she's already doing it? Already using the scent to . . . influence people?"

"You?" Beatrice asked.

"All of us. A group of DGDs. We all live together. We're all controlled, of course, but . . . " Beatrice smiled. "It's probably the quietest house full of kids that anyone's ever seen."

I looked at Alan, and he looked away. "I'm not doing anything to them," I said. "I remind them of work they've already promised to do. That's all."

"You put them at ease," Beatrice said. "You're there. You . . . well, you leave your scent around the house. You speak to them individually. Without knowing why, they no doubt find that very comforting. Don't you, Alan?"

"I don't know," he said. "I suppose I must have. From my first visit to the house, I knew I wanted to move in. And when I first saw Lynn, I . . . " He shook his head. "Funny, I thought all that was my idea."

"Will you work with us, Alan?"

"Me? You want Lynn."

"I want you both. You have no idea how many people take one look at one workroom here and turn and run. You may be the kind of young people who ought to eventually take charge of a place like Dilg."

"Whether we want to or not, eh?" he said.

Frightened, I tried to take his hand, but he moved it away. "Alan, this works," I said. "It's only a stopgap, I know. Genetic engineering will probably give us the final answers, but for God's sake, this is something we can do now!"

"It's something *you* can do. Play queen bee in a retreat full of workers. I've never had any ambition to be a drone."

"A physician isn't likely to be a drone," Beatrice said.

"Would you marry one of your patients?" he demanded. "That's what Lynn would be doing if she married me—whether I become a doctor or not."

She looked away from him, stared across the room. "My husband is here," she said softly. "He's been a patient here for almost a decade. What better place for him . . . when his time came?"

"Shit!" Alan muttered. He glanced at me. "Let's get out of here!" He got up and strode across the room to the door, pulled at it, then realized it was locked. He turned to face Beatrice, his body language demanding she let him out. She went to him, took him by the shoulder, and turned him to face the door. "Try it once more," she said quietly. "You can't break it. Try."

Surprisingly, some of the hostility seemed to go out of him. "This is one of those p.v. locks?" he asked.

"Yes."

I set my teeth and looked away. Let her work. She knew how to use this thing she and I both had. And for the moment, she was on my side.

I heard him make some effort with the door. The door didn't even rattle. Beatrice took his hand from it, and with her own hand flat against what appeared to be a large brass knob, she pushed the door open.

"The man who created that lock is nobody in particular," she said. "He doesn't have an unusually high I.Q., didn't even finish college. But sometime in his life he read a science-fiction story in which palmprint locks were a given. He went that story one better by creating one that responded to voice or palm. It took him years, but we were able to give him those years. The people of Dilg are problem solvers, Alan. Think of the problems you could solve!"

He looked as though he were beginning to think, beginning to understand. "I don't see how biological research can be done that way," he said. "Not with everyone acting on his own, not even aware of other researchers and their work."

"It *is* being done," she said, "and not in isolation. Our retreat in Colorado specializes in it and has—just barely—enough trained, controlled DGDs to see that no one really works in isolation. Our patients can still read and write—those who haven't damaged themselves too badly. They can take each other's work into account if reports are made available to them. And they can read material that comes in from the outside. They're working, Alan. The disease hasn't stopped them, *won't* stop them." He stared at her, seemed to be caught by her intensity—or her scent. He spoke as though his words were a strain, as though they hurt his throat. "I won't be a puppet. I won't be controlled . . . by a goddamn smell!"

"Alan—"

"I won't be what my mother is. I'd rather be dead!"

"There's no reason for you to become what your mother is."

He drew back in obvious disbelief.

"Your mother is brain damaged—thanks to the three months she spent in that custodial-care toilet. She had no speech at all when I met her. She's improved more than you can imagine. None of that has to happen to you. Work with us, and we'll see that none of it happens to you."

He hesitated, seemed less sure of himself. Even that much flexibility in him was surprising. "I'll be under your control or Lynn's," he said.

She shook her head. "Not even your mother is under my control. She's aware of me. She's able to take direction from me. She trusts me the way any blind person would trust her guide."

"There's more to it than that."

"Not here. Not at any of our retreats."

"I don't believe you."

"Then you don't understand how much individuality our people retain. They know they need help, but they have minds of their own. If you want to see the abuse of power you're worried about, go to a DGD ward."

"You're better than that, I admit. Hell is probably better than that. But . . ."

"But you don't trust us."

He shrugged.

"You do, you know." She smiled. "You don't want to, but you do. That's what worries you, and it leaves you with work to do. Look into what I've said. See for yourself. We offer DGDs a chance to live and do whatever they decide is important to them. What do you have, what can you realistically hope for that's better than that?"

Silence. "I don't know what to think," he said finally.

"Go home," she said. "Decide what to think. It's the most important decision you'll ever make."

He looked at me. I went to him, not sure how he'd react, not sure he'd want me no matter what he decided.

"What are you going to do?" he asked.

The question startled me. "You have a choice," I said. "I don't. If she's right . . . how could I not wind up running a retreat?"

"Do you want to?"

I swallowed. I hadn't really faced that question yet. Did I want to spend my life in something that was basically a refined DGD ward? "No!"

"But you will."

" . . . Yes." I thought for a moment, hunted for the right words. "You'd do it."

"What?"

"If the pheromone were something only men had, you would do it."

That silence again. After a time he took my hand, and we followed Beatrice out to the car. Before I could get in with him and our guard-escort, she caught my arm. I jerked away reflexively. By the time I caught myself, I had swung around as though I meant to hit her. Hell, I did mean to hit her, but I stopped myself in time. "Sorry," I said with no attempt at sincerity.

She held out a card until I took it. "My private number," she said. "Before seven or after nine, usually. You and I will communicate best by phone."

I resisted the impulse to throw the card away. God, she brought out the child in me.

Inside the car, Alan said something to the guard. I couldn't hear what it was, but the sound of his voice reminded me of him arguing with her—her logic and her scent. She had all but won him for me, and I couldn't manage even token gratitude. I spoke to her, low voiced.

"He never really had a chance, did he?"

She looked surprised. "That's up to you. You can keep him or drive him away. I assure you, you *can* drive him away."

"How?"

"By imagining that he doesn't have a chance." She smiled faintly. "Phone me from your territory. We have a great deal to say to each other, and I'd rather we didn't say it as enemies."

She had lived with meeting people like me for decades. She had good control. I, on the other hand, was at the end of my control. All I could do was scramble into the car and floor my own phantom accelerator as the guard drove us to the gate. I couldn't look back at her. Until we were well away from the house, until we'd left the guard at the gate and gone off the property, I couldn't make myself look back. For long, irrational minutes, I was convinced that somehow if I turned, I would see myself standing there, gray and old, growing small in the distance, vanishing.

Afterword

"The Evening and the Morning and the Night" grew from my ongoing fascinations with biology, medicine, and personal responsibility.

In particular, I began the story wondering how much of what we do is encouraged, discouraged, or otherwise guided by what we are genetically. This is one of my favorite questions, parent to several of my novels. It can be a dangerous question. All too often, when people ask it, they mean who has the biggest or the best or the most of whatever they see as desirable, or who has the smallest and the least of what is undesirable. Genetics as a board game, or worse, as an excuse for the social Darwinism that swings into popularity every few years. Nasty habit.

And yet the question itself is fascinating. And disease, grim as it is, is one way to explore answers. Genetic disorders in particular may teach us much about who and what we are.

I built Duryea-Gode disease from elements of three genetic disorders. The first is Huntington's disease—hereditary, dominant, and thus an inevitability if one has the gene for it. And it is caused by only one abnormal gene. Also Huntington's does not usually show itself until its sufferers are middle-aged.

In addition to Huntington's, I used phenylketonuria (PKU), a recessive genetic disorder that causes severe mental impairment unless the infant who has it is put on a special diet.

Finally, I used Lesch-Nyhan disease, which causes both mental impairment and self-mutilation.

To elements of these disorders, I added my own particular twists: a sensitivity to pheromones and the sufferers' persistent delusion that they are trapped, imprisoned within their own flesh, and that that flesh is somehow not truly part of them. In that last, I took an idea familiar to us all—present in many religions and philosophies—and carried it to a terrible extreme.

We carry as many as 50,000 different genes in each of the nuclei of our billions of cells. If one gene among the 50,000, the Huntington's gene, for instance, can so greatly change our lives—what we can do, what we can become—then what are we?

What, indeed?

For readers who find this question as fascinating as I do, I offer a brief, unconventional reading list: *The Chimpanzees of Gombe: Patterns of Behavior* by Jane Goodall, *The Boy Who Couldn't Stop Washing: The Experience and Treatment of Obsessive-Compulsive Disorder* by Judith L. Rapoport, *Medical Detectives* by Berton Roueché, *An Anthropologist on Mars: Seven Paradoxical Tales* and *The Man Who Mistook His Wife for a Hat and Other Clinical Tales* by Oliver Sacks.

Enjoy!

Near of Kin

"She wanted you," my uncle said. "She didn't have to have a child, you know. Not even twenty-two years ago."

"I know." I sat down opposite him in a comfortable wooden rocking chair in the living room of my mother's apartment. At my feet were papers stuffed into a large cardboard lettuce box—papers loose and dog-eared, flat and enveloped, important and trivial, all jumbled together. Here was her marriage certificate, the deed to property she'd owned in Oregon, a handmade card done in green and red crayon on cheap age-darkened paper— "To Mama," it said. "Merry Christmas." I had made it when I was six and given it to my grandmother whom I called mama then. Now I wondered whether my grandmother had passed it on to my mother along with a kindly lie.

"She was widowed just before you were born," my uncle said. "She just couldn't face caring for a child all alone."

"People do it all the time," I said.

"She wasn't 'people,' she was herself. She knew what she could handle and what she couldn't. She saw to it that you had a good home with your grandmother."

I looked at him, wondering why he still bothered to defend her. What difference did it make now what I felt for her—or didn't feel. "I remember when I was about eight," I said. "She came to see me, and I asked if I could stay with her for awhile. She said I couldn't, said she had to work, didn't have room, didn't have enough money, and a lot of other things. The message I got was that she didn't want to be bothered with me. So I asked her if she was really my mother or if maybe I was adopted."

My uncle winced. "What did she say?"

"Nothing. She hit me."

He sighed. "That temper of hers. She was too nervous, too high-strung. That was one of the reasons she left you with your grandmother."

"What were the others?"

"I think you just listed them. Lack of money, space, time . . . "

"Patience, love . . . "

My uncle shrugged. "Is that what you wanted to talk to me about? All your reasons for disliking your mother?"

"No."

"Well?"

I stared at the box on the floor. The bottom of it had broken with the weight of the papers when I took it from my mother's closet. Maybe there was masking tape somewhere in the apartment. I got up to look, thinking my uncle might get tired of my silence and leave. He did that sometimes—his own quiet form of impatience. It used to scare me when I was little. Now, I would have almost welcomed it. If he left, I wouldn't have to tell him what I wanted to talk to him about . . . yet. He had always been a friend as well as a relative—my mother's five-years-older brother, and the only relative other than my grandmother who'd ever paid more than passing attention to me. He used to talk to me sometimes at my grandmother's house. He treated me like a little adult, because in spite of all the children his married brothers and sisters had, no one had ever convinced him that children were not little adults. He put a lot of pressure on me without realizing he was doing it, but still, I preferred him to the other aunts and uncles, to the old ladies who were my grandmother's friends, to anyone who had ever patted me on the head and told me to be a good little girl. I got along better with him than I had with my mother, so even now, especially now, I didn't want to lose him.

He was still there when I found the tape in a kitchen drawer. He hadn't moved except to take a paper out of the box. He sat reading it while I struggled to tape the box. It was awkward, but I didn't expect him to help me unless I asked—any other male relative, perhaps, but not him.

"What is that?" I asked, glancing at the paper.

"One of your report cards. Fifth grade. Bad."

"Oh God. Throw it out."

"Don't you wonder why she kept it?"

"No. She . . . I think I understood her a little. I think she liked having had a child—I don't know, to prove her womanliness or something, and to see what she could produce. But once she had me, she didn't want to waste her time raising me."

"She had had four miscarriages before you, you know."

"She told me."

"And she did pay attention to you."

"Sometimes. Like whenever I got one of those rotten report cards, she would come over and bawl me out."

"Is that why you got them? To make her angry?"

"I got them because I didn't care one way or the other—until the day you came over and bawled me out and scared the hell out of me. Then I started to care."

"Wait a moment, I remember that. I wasn't trying to scare you. I just thought you had a brain and weren't using it, and I told you so."

"You did. You sat there looking angry and disgusted, and I was afraid you'd given up on me altogether." I glanced at him. "You see? Even if I wasn't adopted, you were. I had to make sure I hung on to you."

That got as much of a smile out of him as anything ever did, and the smile took years off him. He was fifty-seven now, slender, fine boned, still handsome. Everyone in my mother's family was that way—small, almost fragile looking. It made the women attractive. I thought it made the men attractive too, but I knew it had caused my male cousins to spend too much of their time fighting and showing off, trying to prove they were men. It had made them touchy and defensive. I don't know what it had done to this particular uncle when he was a boy, but he wasn't defensive now. If you made him angry, he could deliver an icy verbal shredding. If that wasn't enough, he could handle himself in a fight too—or he could when he was younger—but I had never seen him start trouble. My cousins disliked him, claimed he was ice-cold even when he wasn't angry. When I disagreed with them, they told me I was cold too. What difference did it make? My uncle and I got along comfortably together.

"What are you going to do with her things?" he asked.

"Sell them, give them to the Salvation Army, I don't know. Do you see anything you want?"

He got up and went into the bedroom, moving with that smooth, quick grace of his that time didn't seem to touch. He came back with a picture from my mother's dresser—an enlargement of a snapshot he had taken of my mother, grandmother, and me at Knott's Berry Farm when I was about twelve. Somehow, he had gotten us together and taken us all out for a treat. The picture was the only one I knew of that contained the three of us.

"It would have been better if you had gotten into that photo too," I said. "You should have had some stranger take the picture."

"No, you three look right together—three generations. Are you sure you don't want to keep this picture—or a copy of it?"

I shook my head. "It's yours. Don't you want anything else?"

"No. What are you going to do about that Oregon property? And I think she owned some in Arizona, too."

"Everywhere but here," I muttered. "After all, if she'd used her money to buy a house here, I might have moved in on her. Where did all that money come from anyway? She was supposed to be so damn poor!"

"She's dead," said my uncle flatly. "How much more time and energy are you going to waste resenting her?"

"As little as possible," I said. "I can't quite turn it off like a water faucet though."

"Turn it off when I'm around. She was my sister and I loved her if you didn't." He said it very quietly, mildly.

"Okay."

There was a silence until one of my aunts arrived. She hugged me when I let her in and cried all over me. I endured her because my mother had been her sister, too. She was a tiresome woman who used to visit my grandmother to talk about how gifted her own kids were while she patted me on the head and treated me like the family idiot.

"Stephen," she greeted my uncle. He hated his first name. "What do you have there? A picture. Isn't that nice. Barbara was so pretty then. She was always a beauty. So natural at the funeral . . ."

She wandered into the bedroom and began going through my mother's things. At the closet, she sighed. She was at least twenty pounds heavier than my mother, though I could remember when they were the same size.

"What are you going to do with all these lovely things?" she asked me. "You should save some of them as keepsakes."

"Should I?" I said. I was going to get rid of all of them as soon as possible, of course—bundle them off to the Salvation Army. But this aunt, who had disapproved self-righteously of my mother's unmotherly behavior for years, would be outraged now if I seemed unsentimental about my mother's things.

"Stephen, are you helping out?" my aunt asked.

"No," said my uncle softly.

"Just keeping company, hmm? That's nice. Is there anything I can do?"

"Nothing," said my uncle—which was strange because the question had clearly been directed at me. She looked at him a little surprised, and he looked back expressionlessly.

"Well . . . if you need me for anything, you be sure and call me." She had gathered up a few pieces of my mother's jewelry. Now she grabbed the little black-and-white television. "You don't mind if I take this, do you? My younger kids fight so much over the TV. . . ." She left.

My uncle looked after her and shook his head.

"She's your sister, too," I said, smiling.

"If she wasn't . . . Never mind."

"What?"

"Nothing." That soft warning voice again. I ignored it.

"I know. She's a hypocrite—among other things. I think she liked my mother even less than I did."

"Why did you let her take those things?"

I looked at him. "Because I don't care what happens to anything in this apartment. I just don't care."

"Well . . . " He took a deep breath. "You're no hypocrite, at least. Your mother left a will, you know."

"A will?"

"That property is fairly valuable. She left it to you."

"How do you know?"

"I have a copy of the will. She didn't trust anyone to find it in her things." He waved a hand toward the cardboard box. "Her brand of filing wasn't very dependable."

I nodded unhappily. "It sure wasn't. I don't have any idea what she has here. But look, isn't there any way you could take that property? I don't want it."

"She wanted to do something for you. Let her do it."

"But . . . "

"Let her do it."

I drew a deep breath, then let it out. "Did she leave you anything?"

"No."

"That doesn't seem right."

"I'm content—or I will be when you take what she's given you. There's some money, too."

I frowned, unable to imagine my mother saving any money. I hadn't even found out about the property until I began going through her things. The money was a little too much. But, at least, it gave me the opening I needed. "Is this money from her," I asked him, "or from you?"

He hesitated just for a second, then said, "It's in her will." But there was something wrong with the way he said it—as though I'd caught him a little off guard.

I smiled, but stopped when that seemed to make him uncomfortable. I didn't want to make him uncomfortable. I was going to—I had to—but I didn't look forward to it or take any pleasure in it.

"You're not devious," I told him. "You look as though you could be. You look secretive and controlled."

"I can't help the way I look."

"People tell me I look that way, too."

"No, you look like your mother."

"I think not. I think I look like my father."

He said nothing, just stared at me, frowning. I fingered a few of the dog-eared papers in the box. "Shall I still take the money?"

He did not answer. He only watched me in that way of his that people called cold. It wasn't—I knew what he was like when he was really cold. Now, it was more as though he were in pain, as though I were hurting him. I supposed I was, but I couldn't stop. It was too late to stop. I pressed my fingers nervously into the jumble of papers, then looked down at them for a moment, suddenly resenting them. Why hadn't I stayed at college and left them, left everything to other relatives the way she had always left me to other relatives? Or, having come here like a responsible daughter to wind up my mother's affairs, why hadn't I done just that and kept my mouth shut? What would he do now? Leave? Would I lose him, too?

"I don't care," I said not looking at him. "It doesn't matter. I love you." I had said that to him before dozens of times, obscurely. But I had never said it in just those three words. It was as though I were asking permission somehow. *Is it all right for me to love you?*

"What have you got in that box?" he asked softly.

I frowned for a moment, not understanding. Then I realized what he thought—what my nervousness had made him think. "Nothing about this," I said, "at least nothing that I know of. Don't worry, I don't think she would have written anything down."

"Then how did you know?"

"I didn't know, I guessed. I guessed a long time ago."

"How?"

I kicked at the box. "There were a lot of things," I said. "I guess the easiest one to explain is the way we look, you and I. You should compare one of Grandmother's pictures of you as a young man with my face now—we could be twins. My mother was beautiful; her husband, from his pictures, was a big, handsome man—me . . . I just look like you."

"That doesn't have to mean anything."

"I know. But it meant a lot to me, together with some other less tangible things."

"A guess," he said bitterly. He leaned forward. "I'm really not very devious, am I?" He stood up, started toward the door. I got up quickly to block his way. We were the same height, exactly.

"Please don't go," I said. "Please."

He tried to put me aside gently, but I wouldn't move.

"Say it?" I insisted. "I'll never ask you again, nor will I ever repeat it. She's dead; it can't hurt her anymore." I hesitated. "Please don't walk away from me."

He sighed, looked at the floor for a moment, then at me. "Yes," he said softly.

I let him go and found myself almost crying with relief. I had a father, then. I didn't feel as though I'd ever had a mother, but I had a father. "Thank you," I whispered.

"No one knows," he said. "Not your grandmother, not any of the relatives."

"They won't find out from me."

"No. I never worried about your telling others. I never worried about others except for the pain they might cause her and you—and the pain it might cause you . . . to know."

"I'm not in pain."

"No." He looked at me with what seemed to be amazement and I realized that he had been at least as frightened as I had.

"How did she have her husband's name put on my birth certificate?" I asked.

"By lying. It was a believable lie—her husband was alive when you were conceived. He had left her, but the family didn't find out about that until later, never found out about the timing."

"Did he leave because of you?"

"No. He left because he had found someone else—someone who had borne him a live child instead of having a miscarriage. She came to me when he left—came to talk, to cry, to work out some of her feelings. . . . " He shrugged. "She and I were always close—too close." He shrugged again. "We loved each other. If it had been possible, I would have married her. I don't care how that sounds, I would have done it. As it was, we were afraid when she realized she was pregnant, but she wanted you. There was never any question about that."

I didn't believe him, even now. I believed what I had said before—that she had wanted a child to prove she was woman enough to have one. Once she had her proof, she went on to other things. But he had loved her and I loved him. I said nothing.

"She was always afraid you would find out," he said. "That was why she couldn't bring herself to keep you with her."

"She was ashamed of me."

"She was ashamed of herself."

I looked at him, trying to read his unreadable face. "Were you?"

He nodded. "Of myself—never of you."

"But you didn't just drop me the way she did."

"She didn't drop you either; she couldn't. Why do you think she was so upset when you asked her if you were adopted?"

I shook my head. "She should have trusted me. She should have been more like you."

"She did the best she could as herself."

"I would have loved her. I wouldn't have cared."

"Knowing you, I think you might not have. She couldn't quite believe that though. She couldn't take the chance."

"Do you love me?"

"Yes. So did she, though you don't believe it."

"She and I . . . we should have gotten to know each other. We never did, really."

"No." There was silence, and he looked over at the box of papers. "If you find anything in there that you can't handle, bring it to me."

"All right."

"I'll call you about the will. Are you going back to school?"

"Yes."

He gave me one of his small smiles. "Then you'll need the money, won't you? I don't want to hear any more nonsense about your not taking it." He left, closing the door silently behind him.

Afterword

First of all, "Near of Kin" has *nothing* to do with my novel *Kindred.* I said this to the editor who originally accepted the story for his anthology, but all he remembered was that I had two works with similar titles, and therefore, they must be related. Not at all.

"Near of Kin" grew from my Baptist childhood and my habit, even then, of letting my interests lead me wherever they would. As a good Baptist kid, I read the Bible first as a series of instructions as to how I should believe and behave, then as bits of verse that I was required to memorize, then as a series of interesting, interconnected stories.

The stories got me: stories of conflict, betrayal, torture, murder, exile, and incest. I read them avidly. This was, of course, not exactly what my mother had in mind when she encouraged me to read the Bible. Nevertheless, I found these things fascinating, and when I began writing, I explored these themes in my own stories. "Near of Kin" is one of the odder results of this interest. I remember trying to write it when I was in college, and failing. The idea stayed with me, demanding to be written: A sympathetic story of incest. My examples were Lot's daughters, Abraham's sister-wife, and the sons of Adam with the daughters of Eve.

Speech Sounds

There was trouble aboard the Washington Boulevard bus. Rye had expected trouble sooner or later in her journey. She had put off going until loneliness and hopelessness drove her out. She believed she might have one group of relatives left alive—a brother and his two children twenty miles away in Pasadena. That was a day's journey one-way, if she were lucky. The unexpected arrival of the bus as she left her Virginia Road home had seemed to be a piece of luck—until the trouble began.

Two young men were involved in a disagreement of some kind, or, more likely, a misunderstanding. They stood in the aisle, grunting and gesturing at each other, each in his own uncertain T stance as the bus lurched over the potholes. The driver seemed to be putting some effort into keeping them off balance. Still, their gestures stopped just short of contact—mock punches, hand games of intimidation to replace lost curses.

People watched the pair, then looked at one another and made small anxious sounds. Two children whimpered.

Rye sat a few feet behind the disputants and across from the back door. She watched the two carefully, knowing the fight would begin when someone's nerve broke or someone's hand slipped or someone came to the end of his limited ability to communicate. These things could happen anytime.

One of them happened as the bus hit an especially large pothole and one man, tall, thin, and sneering, was thrown into his shorter opponent.

Instantly, the shorter man drove his left fist into the disintegrating sneer. He hammered his larger opponent as though he neither had nor needed any weapon other than his left fist. He hit quickly enough, hard enough to batter his opponent down before the taller man could regain his balance or hit back even once.

People screamed or squawked in fear. Those nearby scrambled to get out of the way. Three more young men roared in excitement and gestured wildly. Then, somehow, a second dispute broke out between two of these three—probably because one inadvertently touched or hit the other.

As the second fight scattered frightened passengers, a woman shook the driver's shoulder and grunted as she gestured toward the fighting.

The driver grunted back through bared teeth. Frightened, the woman drew away.

Rye, knowing the methods of bus drivers, braced herself and held on to the crossbar of the seat in front of her. When the driver hit the brakes, she was ready and the combatants were not. They fell over seats and onto screaming passengers, creating even more confusion. At least one more fight started.

The instant the bus came to a full stop, Rye was on her feet, pushing the back door. At the second push, it opened and she jumped out, holding her pack in one arm. Several other passengers followed, but some stayed on the bus. Buses were so rare and irregular now, people rode when they could, no matter what. There might not be another bus today—or tomorrow. People started walking, and if they saw a bus they flagged it down. People making intercity trips like Rye's from Los Angeles to Pasadena made plans to camp out, or risked seeking shelter with locals who might rob or murder them.

The bus did not move, but Rye moved away from it. She intended to wait until the trouble was over and get on again, but if there was shooting, she wanted the protection of a tree. Thus, she was near the curb when a battered blue Ford on the other side of the street made a U-turn and pulled up in front of the bus. Cars were rare these days—as rare as a severe shortage of fuel and of relatively unimpaired mechanics could make them. Cars that still ran were as likely to be used as weapons as they were to serve as transportation. Thus, when the driver of the Ford beckoned to Rye, she moved away warily. The driver got out—a big man, young, neatly bearded with dark, thick hair. He wore a long overcoat and a look of wariness that matched Rye's. She stood several feet from him, waiting to see what he would do. He looked at the bus, now rocking with the combat inside, then at the small cluster of passengers who had gotten off. Finally he looked at Rye again.

She returned his gaze, very much aware of the old forty-five automatic her jacket concealed. She watched his hands.

He pointed with his left hand toward the bus. The dark-tinted windows prevented him from seeing what was happening inside.

His use of the left hand interested Rye more than his obvious question. Left-handed people tended to be less impaired, more reasonable and comprehending, less driven by frustration, confusion, and anger.

She imitated his gesture, pointing toward the bus with her own left hand, then punching the air with both fists.

The man took off his coat revealing a Los Angeles Police Department uniform complete with baton and service revolver.

Rye took another step back from him. There was no more LAPD, no more *any* large organization, governmental or private. There were neighborhood patrols and armed individuals. That was all.

The man took something from his coat pocket, then threw the coat into the car. Then he gestured Rye back, back toward the rear of the bus. He had something made of plastic in his hand. Rye did not understand what he wanted until he went to the rear door of the bus and beckoned her to stand there. She obeyed mainly out of curiosity. Cop or not, maybe he could do something to stop the stupid fighting.

He walked around the front of the bus, to the street side where the driver's window was open. There, she thought she saw him throw something into the bus. She was still trying to peer through the tinted glass when people began stumbling out the rear door, choking and weeping. Gas.

Rye caught an old woman who would have fallen, lifted two little children down when they were in danger of being knocked down and trampled. She could see the bearded man helping people at the front door. She caught a thin old man shoved out by one of the combatants. Staggered by the old man's weight, she was barely able to get out of the way as the last of the young men pushed his way out. This one, bleeding from nose and mouth, stumbled into another, and they grappled blindly, still sobbing from the gas.

The bearded man helped the bus driver out through the front door, though the driver did not seem to appreciate his help. For a moment, Rye thought there would be another fight. The bearded man stepped back and watched the driver gesture threateningly, watched him shout in wordless anger.

The bearded man stood still, made no sound, refused to respond to clearly obscene gestures. The least impaired people tended to do this—stand back unless they were physically threatened and let those with less control scream and jump around. It was as though they felt it beneath them to be as touchy as the less comprehending. This was an attitude of superiority, and that was the way people like the bus driver perceived it. Such "superiority" was frequently punished by beatings, even by death. Rye had had close calls of her own. As a result, she never went unarmed. And in this world where the only likely common language was body language, being armed was often enough. She had rarely had to draw her gun or even display it.

The bearded man's revolver was on constant display. Apparently that was enough for the bus driver. The driver spat in disgust, glared at the bearded man for a moment longer, then strode back to his gas-filled bus. He stared at it for a moment, clearly wanting to get in, but the gas was still too strong. Of the windows, only his tiny driver's window actually opened. The front door was open, but the rear door would not stay open unless someone held it. Of course, the air conditioning had failed long ago. The bus would take some time to clear. It was the driver's property, his livelihood. He had pasted old magazine pictures of items he would accept as fare on its sides. Then he would use what he collected to feed his family or to trade. If his bus did not run, he did not eat. On the other hand, if the inside of his bus was torn apart by senseless fighting, he would not eat very well either. He was apparently unable to perceive this. All he could see was that it would be some time before he could use his bus again. He shook his fist at the bearded man and shouted. There seemed to be words in his shout, but Rye could not understand them. She did not know whether this was his fault or hers. She had heard so little coherent human speech for the past three years, she was no longer certain how well she recognized it, no longer certain of the degree of her own impairment.

The bearded man sighed. He glanced toward his car, then beckoned to Rye. He was ready to leave, but he wanted something from her first. No. No, he wanted her to leave with him. Risk getting into his car when, in spite of his uniform, law and order were nothing—not even words any longer.

She shook her head in a universally understood negative, but the man continued to beckon.

She waved him away. He was doing what the less impaired rarely did—drawing potentially negative attention to another of his kind. People from the bus had begun to look at her.

One of the men who had been fighting tapped another on the arm, then pointed from the bearded man to Rye, and finally held up the first two fingers of his right hand as though giving two-thirds of a Boy Scout salute. The gesture was very quick, its meaning obvious even at a distance. She had been grouped with the bearded man. Now what?

The man who had made the gesture started toward her.

She had no idea what he intended, but she stood her ground. The man was half a foot taller than she was and perhaps ten years younger. She did not imagine she could outrun him. Nor did she expect anyone to help her if she needed help. The people around her were all strangers.

She gestured once—a clear indication to the man to stop. She did not intend to repeat the gesture. Fortunately, the man obeyed. He gestured obscenely and several other men laughed. Loss of verbal language had spawned a whole new set of obscene gestures. The man, with stark simplicity, had accused her of sex with the bearded man and had suggested she accommodate the other men present—beginning with him.

Rye watched him wearily. People might very well stand by and watch if he tried to rape her. They would also stand and watch her shoot him. Would he push things that far?

He did not. After a series of obscene gestures that brought him no closer to her, he turned contemptuously and walked away.

And the bearded man still waited. He had removed his service revolver, holster and all. He beckoned again, both hands empty. No doubt his gun was in the car and within easy reach, but his taking it off impressed her. Maybe he was all right. Maybe he was just alone. She had been alone herself for three years. The illness had stripped her, killing her children one by one, killing her husband, her sister, her parents. . . .

The illness, if it was an illness, had cut even the living off from one another. As it swept over the country, people hardly had time to lay blame on the Soviets (though they were falling silent along with the rest of the world), on a new virus, a new pollutant, radiation, divine retribution. . . . The illness was stroke-swift in the way it cut people down and strokelike in some of its effects. But it was highly specific. Language was always lost or severely impaired. It was never regained. Often there was also paralysis, intellectual impairment, death.

Rye walked toward the bearded man, ignoring the whistling and applauding of two of the young men and their thumbs-up signs to the bearded man. If he had smiled at them or acknowledged them in any way, she would almost certainly have changed her mind. If she had let herself think of the possible deadly consequences of getting into a stranger's car, she would have changed her mind. Instead, she thought of the man who lived across the street from her. He rarely washed since his bout with the illness. And he had gotten into the habit of urinating wherever he happened to be. He had two women already—one tending each of his large gardens. They put up with him in exchange for his protection. He had made it clear that he wanted Rye to become his third woman.

She got into the car and the bearded man shut the door. She watched as he walked around to the driver's door—watched for his sake because his gun was on the seat beside her. And the bus driver and a pair of young men had come a few steps closer. They did nothing, though, until the bearded man was in the car. Then one of them threw a rock. Others followed his example, and as the car drove away, several rocks bounced off harmlessly.

When the bus was some distance behind them, Rye wiped sweat from her forehead and longed to relax. The bus would have taken her more than halfway to Pasadena. She would have had only ten miles to walk. She wondered how far she would have to walk now—and wondered if walking a long distance would be her only problem.

At Figuroa and Washington where the bus normally made a left turn, the bearded man stopped, looked at her, and indicated that she should choose a direction. When she directed him left and he actually turned left, she began to relax. If he was willing to go where she directed, perhaps he was safe.

As they passed blocks of burned, abandoned buildings, empty lots, and wrecked or stripped cars, he slipped a gold chain over his head and handed it to her. The pendant attached to it was a smooth, glassy, black rock. Obsidian. His name might be Rock or Peter or Black, but she decided to think of him as Obsidian. Even her sometimes useless memory would retain a name like Obsidian.

She handed him her own name symbol—a pin in the shape of a large golden stalk of wheat. She had bought it long before the illness and the silence began. Now she wore it, thinking it was as close as she was likely to come to Rye. People like Obsidian who had not known her before probably thought of her as Wheat. Not that it mattered. She would never hear her name spoken again.

Obsidian handed her pin back to her. He caught her hand as she reached for it and rubbed his thumb over her calluses.

He stopped at First Street and asked which way again. Then, after turning right as she had indicated, he parked near the Music Center. There, he took a folded paper from the dashboard and unfolded it. Rye recognized it as a street map, though the writing on it meant nothing to her. He flattened the map, took her hand again, and put her index finger on one spot. He touched her, touched himself, pointed toward the floor. In effect, "We are here." She knew he wanted to know where she was going. She wanted to tell him, but she shook her head sadly. She had lost reading and writing. That was her most serious impairment and her most painful. She had taught history at UCLA. She had done freelance writing. Now she could not even read her own manuscripts. She had a houseful of books that she could neither read nor bring herself to use as fuel. And she had a memory that would not bring back to her much of what she had read before.

She stared at the map, trying to calculate. She had been born in Pasadena, had lived for fifteen years in Los Angeles. Now she was near L.A. Civic Center. She knew the relative positions of the two cities, knew streets, directions, even knew to stay away from freeways, which might be blocked by wrecked cars and destroyed overpasses. She ought to know how to point out Pasadena even though she could not recognize the word.

Hesitantly, she placed her hand over a pale orange patch in the upper right corner of the map. That should be right. Pasadena.

Obsidian lifted her hand and looked under it, then folded the map and put it back on the dashboard. He could read, she realized belatedly. He could probably write, too. Abruptly, she hated him—deep, bitter hatred. What did literacy mean to him—a grown man who played cops and robbers? But he was literate and she was not. She never would be. She felt sick to her stomach with hatred, frustration, and jealousy. And only a few inches from her hand was a loaded gun.

She held herself still, staring at him, almost seeing his blood. But her rage crested and ebbed and she did nothing.

Obsidian reached for her hand with hesitant familiarity. She looked at him. Her face had already revealed too much. No person still living in what was left of human society could fail to recognize that expression, that jealousy.

She closed her eyes wearily, drew a deep breath. She had experienced longing for the past, hatred of the present, growing hopelessness, purposelessness, but she had never experienced such a powerful urge to kill another person. She had left her home, finally, because she had come near to killing herself. She had found no reason to stay alive. Perhaps that was why she had gotten into Obsidian's car. She had never before done such a thing.

He touched her mouth and made chatter motions with thumb and fingers. Could she speak?

She nodded and watched his milder envy come and go. Now both had admitted what it was not safe to admit, and there had been no violence. He tapped his mouth and forehead and shook his head. He did not speak or comprehend spoken language. The illness had played with them, taking away, she suspected, what each valued most.

She plucked at his sleeve, wondering why he had decided on his own to keep the LAPD alive with what he had left. He was sane enough otherwise. Why wasn't he at home raising corn, rabbits, and children? But she did not know how to ask. Then he put his hand on her thigh and she had another question to deal with.

She shook her head. Disease, pregnancy, helpless, solitary agony . . . no.

He massaged her thigh gently and smiled in obvious disbelief.

No one had touched her for three years. She had not wanted anyone to touch her. What kind of world was this to chance bringing a child into even if the father were willing to stay and help raise it? It was too bad, though. Obsidian could not know how attractive he was to her—young, probably younger than she was, clean, asking for what he wanted rather than demanding it. But none of that mattered. What were a few moments of pleasure measured against a lifetime of consequences?

He pulled her closer to him and for a moment she let herself enjoy the closeness. He smelled good—male and good. She pulled away reluctantly.

He sighed, reached toward the glove compartment. She stiffened, not knowing what to expect, but all he took out was a small box. The writing on it meant nothing to her. She did not understand until he broke the seal, opened the box, and took out a condom. He looked at her, and she first looked away in surprise. Then she giggled. She could not remember when she had last giggled.

He grinned, gestured toward the backseat, and she laughed aloud. Even in her teens, she had disliked backseats of cars. But she looked around at the empty streets and ruined buildings, then she got out and into the backseat. He let her put the condom on him, then seemed surprised at her eagerness.

Sometime later, they sat together, covered by his coat, unwilling to become clothed near strangers again just yet. He made rock-the-baby gestures and looked questioningly at her.

She swallowed, shook her head. She did not know how to tell him her children were dead.

He took her hand and drew a cross in it with his index finger, then made his baby-rocking gesture again.

She nodded, held up three fingers, then turned away, trying to shut out a sudden flood of memories. She had told herself that the children growing up now were to be pitied. They would run through the downtown canyons with no real memory of what the buildings had been or even how they had come to be. Today's children gathered books as well as wood to be burned as fuel. They ran through the streets chasing one another and hooting like chimpanzees. They had no future. They were now all they would ever be.

He put his hand on her shoulder, and she turned suddenly, fumbling for his small box, then urging him to make love to her again. He could give her forgetfulness and pleasure. Until now, nothing had been able to do that. Until now, every day had brought her closer to the time when she would do what she had left home to avoid doing: putting her gun in her mouth and pulling the trigger.

She asked Obsidian if he would come home with her, stay with her.

He looked surprised and pleased once he understood. But he did not answer at once. Finally, he shook his head as she had feared he might. He was probably having too much fun playing cops and robbers and picking up women.

She dressed in silent disappointment, unable to feel any anger toward him. Perhaps he already had a wife and a home. That was likely. The illness had been harder on men than on women—had killed more men, had left male survivors more severely impaired. Men like Obsidian were rare. Women either settled for less or stayed alone. If they found an Obsidian, they did what they could to keep him. Rye suspected he had someone younger, prettier keeping him.

He touched her while she was strapping her gun on and asked with a complicated series of gestures whether it was loaded.

She nodded grimly.

He patted her arm.

She asked once more if he would come home with her, this time using a different series of gestures. He had seemed hesitant. Perhaps he could be courted.

He got out and into the front seat without responding.

She took her place in front again, watching him. Now he plucked at his uniform and looked at her. She thought she was being asked something but did not know what it was.

He took off his badge, tapped it with one finger, then tapped his chest. Of course.

She took the badge from his hand and pinned her wheat stalk to it. If playing cops and robbers was his only insanity, let him play. She would take him, uniform and all. It occurred to her that she might eventually lose him to someone he would meet as he had met her. But she would have him for a while.

He took the street map down again, tapped it, pointed vaguely northeast toward Pasadena, then looked at her.

She shrugged, tapped his shoulder, then her own, and held up her index and second fingers tight together, just to be sure.

He grasped the two fingers and nodded. He was with her.

She took the map from him and threw it onto the dashboard. She pointed back southwest—back toward home. Now she did not have to go to Pasadena. Now she could go on having a brother there and two nephews—three right-handed males. Now she did not have to find out for certain whether she was as alone as she feared. Now she was not alone.

Obsidian took Hill Street south, then Washington west, and she leaned back, wondering what it would be like to have someone again. With what she had scavenged, what she had preserved, and what she grew, there was easily enough food for them. There was certainly room enough in a four-bedroom house. He could move his possessions in. Best of all, the animal across the street would pull back and possibly not force her to kill him.

Obsidian had drawn her closer to him, and she had put her head on his shoulder when suddenly he braked hard, almost throwing her off the seat. Out of the corner of her eye, she saw that someone had run across the street in front of the car. One car on the street and someone had to run in front of it.

Straightening up, Rye saw that the runner was a woman, fleeing from an old frame house to a boarded-up storefront. She ran silently, but the man who followed her a moment later shouted what sounded like garbled words as he ran. He had something in his hand. Not a gun. A knife, perhaps.

The woman tried a door, found it locked, looked around desperately, finally snatched up a fragment of glass broken from the storefront window. With this she turned to face her pursuer. Rye thought she would be more likely to cut her own hand than to hurt anyone else with the glass.

Obsidian jumped from the car, shouting. It was the first time Rye had heard his voice—deep and hoarse from disuse. He made the same sound over and over the way some speechless people did, "Da, da, da!"

Rye got out of the car as Obsidian ran toward the couple. He had drawn his gun. Fearful, she drew her own and released the safety. She looked around to see who else might be attracted to the scene. She saw the man glance at Obsidian, then suddenly lunge at the woman. The woman jabbed his face with her glass, but he caught her arm and managed to stab her twice before Obsidian shot him.

The man doubled, then toppled, clutching his abdomen. Obsidian shouted, then gestured Rye over to help the woman.

Rye moved to the woman's side, remembering that she had little more than bandages and antiseptic in her pack. But the woman was beyond help. She had been stabbed with a long, slender boning knife.

She touched Obsidian to let him know the woman was dead. He had bent to check the wounded man who lay still and also seemed dead. But as Obsidian looked around to see what Rye wanted, the man opened his eyes. Face contorted, he seized Obsidian's just-holstered revolver and fired. The bullet caught Obsidian in the temple and he collapsed.

It happened just that simply, just that fast. An instant later, Rye shot the wounded man as he was turning the gun on her.

And Rye was alone—with three corpses.

She knelt beside Obsidian, dry-eyed, frowning, trying to understand why everything had suddenly changed. Obsidian was gone. He had died and left her—like everyone else.

Two very small children came out of the house from which the man and woman had run—a boy and girl perhaps three years old. Holding hands, they crossed the street toward Rye. They stared at her, then edged past her and went to the dead woman. The girl shook the woman's arm as though trying to wake her.

This was too much. Rye got up, feeling sick to her stomach with grief and anger. If the children began to cry, she thought she would vomit.

They were on their own, those two kids. They were old enough to scavenge. She did not need any more grief. She did not need a stranger's children who would grow up to be hairless chimps.

She went back to the car. She could drive home, at least. She remembered how to drive.

The thought that Obsidian should be buried occurred to her before she reached the car, and she did vomit.

She had found and lost the man so quickly. It was as though she had been snatched from comfort and security and given a sudden, inexplicable beating. Her head would not clear. She could not think.

Somehow, she made herself go back to him, look at him. She found herself on her knees beside him with no memory of having knelt. She stroked his face, his beard. One of the children made a noise and she looked at them, at the woman who was probably their mother. The children looked back at her, obviously frightened. Perhaps it was their fear that reached her finally.

She had been about to drive away and leave them. She had almost done it, almost left two toddlers to die. Surely there had been enough dying. She would have to take the children home with her. She would not be able to live with any other decision. She looked around for a place to bury three bodies. Or two. She wondered if the murderer were the children's father. Before the silence, the police had always said some of the most dangerous calls they went out on were domestic disturbance calls. Obsidian should have known that—not that the knowledge would have kept him in the car. It would not have held her back either. She could not have watched the woman murdered and done nothing.

She dragged Obsidian toward the car. She had nothing to dig with her, and no one to guard for her while she dug. Better to take the bodies with her and bury them next to her husband and her children. Obsidian would come home with her after all.

When she had gotten him onto the floor in the back, she returned for the woman. The little girl, thin, dirty, solemn, stood up and unknowingly gave Rye a gift. As Rye began to drag the woman by her arms, the little girl screamed, "No!"

Rye dropped the woman and stared at the girl.

"No!" the girl repeated. She came to stand beside the woman. "Go away!" she told Rye.

"Don't talk," the little boy said to her. There was no blurring or confusing of sounds. Both children had spoken and Rye had understood. The boy looked at the dead murderer and moved further from him. He took the girl's hand. "Be quiet," he whispered.

Fluent speech! Had the woman died because she could talk and had taught her children to talk? Had she been killed by a husband's festering anger or by a stranger's jealous rage?

And the children . . . they must have been born after the silence. Had the disease run its course, then? Or were these children simply immune? Certainly they had had time to fall sick and silent. Rye's mind leaped ahead. What if children of three or fewer years were safe and able to learn language? What if all they needed were teachers? Teachers and protectors.

Rye glanced at the dead murderer. To her shame, she thought she could understand some of the passions that must have driven him, whomever he was. Anger, frustration, hopelessness, insane jealousy . . . how many more of him were there—people willing to destroy what they could not have?

Obsidian had been the protector, had chosen that role for who knew what reason. Perhaps putting on an obsolete uniform and patrolling the empty streets had been what he did instead of putting a gun into his mouth. And now that there was something worth protecting, he was gone.

She had been a teacher. A good one. She had been a protector, too, though only of herself. She had kept herself alive when she had no reason to live. If the illness let these children alone, she could keep them alive.

Somehow she lifted the dead woman into her arms and placed her on the backseat of the car. The children began to cry, but she knelt on the broken pavement and whispered to them, fearful of frightening them with the harshness of her long unused voice.

"It's all right," she told them. "You're going with us, too. Come on." She lifted them both, one in each arm. They were so light. Had they been getting enough to eat?

The boy covered her mouth with his hand, but she moved her face away. "It's all right for me to talk," she told him. "As long as no one's around, it's all right." She put the boy down on the front seat of the car and he moved over without being told to, to make room for the girl. When they were both in the car, Rye leaned against the window, looking at them, seeing that they were less afraid now, that they watched her with at least as much curiosity as fear.

"I'm Valerie Rye," she said, savoring the words. "It's all right for you to talk to me."

Afterword

"Speech Sounds" was conceived in weariness, depression, and sorrow. I began the story feeling little hope or liking for the human species, but by the time I reached the end of it, my hope had come back. It always seems to do that. Here's the story behind "Speech Sounds."

In the early 1980s, a good friend of mine discovered that she was dying of multiple myeloma, an especially dangerous, painful form of cancer. I had lost elderly relatives and family friends to death before this, but I had never lost a personal friend. I had never watched a relatively young person die slowly and painfully of disease. It took my friend a year to die, and I got into the habit of visiting her every Saturday and taking along the latest chapter of the novel I was working on. This happened to be *Clay's Ark*. With its story of disease and death, it was thoroughly inappropriate for the situation. But my friend had always read my novels. She insisted that she wanted to read this one as well. I suspect that neither of us believed she would live to read it in its completed form—although, of course, we didn't talk about this.

I hated going to see her. She was a good person, I loved her, and I hated watching her die. Nevertheless, every Saturday I got on a bus—I don't drive—and went to her hospital room or her apartment. She got thinner and frailer and querulous with pain. I got more depressed.

One Saturday, as I sat on a crowded, smelly bus, trying to keep people from stepping on my ingrown toenail and trying not to think of terrible things, I noticed trouble brewing just across from me. One man had decided he didn't like the way another man was looking at him. Didn't like it at all! It's hard to know where to look when you're wedged in place on a crowded bus.

The wedged-in man argued that he hadn't done anything wrong—which he hadn't. He inched toward the exit as though he meant to get himself out of a potentially bad situation. Then he turned and edged back into the argument. Maybe his own pride was involved. Why the hell should he be the one to run away?

This time the other guy decided that it was his girlfriend—sitting next to him—who was being looked at inappropriately. He attacked.

The fight was short and bloody. The rest of us—the other passengers—ducked and yelled and tried to avoid being hit. In the end, the attacker and his girlfriend pushed their way off the bus, fearful that the driver would call the police. And the guy with the pride sagged, dazed and bloody, looking around as though he wasn't sure what had happened.

I sat where I was, more depressed than ever, hating the whole hopeless, stupid business and wondering whether the human species would ever grow up enough to learn to communicate without using fists of one kind or another.

And the first line of a possible story came to me: "There was trouble aboard the Washington Boulevard bus."

Crossover

At work that day, they put her to soldering J9 connectors into a harness, and they expected her to do twice as many as everyone else. She did, of course, but her only reward was resentment from the slower girls down the line because she was making them look bad. At lunch a couple of them came to her solitary corner table and told her to ease off. That was how it was. If she did good work, other employees resented her and her lead man ignored her. If her work fell off, other employees ignored her and her lead man wrote "bad attitude" on her work review. She hadn't had a raise in two years. She would have quit long ago had she not been afraid to try to start all over again at a new place where the people might be even worse.

Through the afternoon all she wanted was two or three aspirins and sleep. She had not had a headache for three months and this one scared her.

As usual, though, she managed to finish the day. When she got off she even felt hungry enough to make a side trip to the store for a can of something for dinner. It was her headache that drove her to make the shorter trip to the liquor store instead of going to the grocery store. *It was her headache.*

The liquor store was on a corner only two blocks from where she worked. It was across from a pool hall and a bar and near a cheap hotel. That made it a gathering place for certain kinds of people.

There was a crowd on the corner when she got there. Besides the usual drunks and prostitutes, there was a group of teenage boys who were bored enough not to ignore her. For a moment they whispered to each other, laughing. Then as she passed them, the calls began.

"Hey, Jeffery, there go your old woman!"

"Lady, you sure shouldn't have let that car run over you face!"

"Hey, lady, this boy say he go for you!"

A wino sidled up to her. "Come on, baby, let's you and me go up to my room."

She jerked herself out of the alcoholic cloud that surrounded him and went into the store. The clerk there was rude to her because he was rude to everyone. He did not matter any more than the others. The wino tried to catch her by the arm as she left.

"Come on, you not in too big a hurry to talk to me. . . ." She almost ran from him, barely controlling her disgust. She left him standing, swaying slightly in the middle of the street, staring after her.

As she neared the hotel she noticed someone standing in the narrow doorway. A man who had something wrong with his face. *Something* . . . She almost turned and went back toward the drunk. But the man stepped out and came over to her during her moment of hesitation. She looked around quickly, her eyes wide with fear. No one was paying any particular attention to her. Even the wino had begun to move away.

The man said, "I don't go away if you ignore me." He had a scar that ran the length of his face from eye to chin on the left side. When he talked or smiled or frowned, it moved and she could watch it and ignore everything else. Sometimes she could even avoid listening to him. Now she watched it and thought quickly.

"So you got out." There was nothing but bitterness in her voice.

He laughed and the scar curved, wormlike. "This morning. I expected you to be there to meet me."

"No you didn't. I told you three months ago you could stay locked up forever as far as I was concerned."

"And you didn't mean it then either. Ninety days. That's a long time."

"You should have thought about that before you got into the fight."

"Yeah. Man hits me and pulls a knife. I had all the time in the world to remember you didn't want me fighting." He paused. "You know, you could have come to see me just once while I was in."

"I'm sorry." Toneless. False without any attempt to hide the falseness.

He made a sound of disgust. "The day you're sorry for anything . . . "

"All right, I'm not sorry. I don't give a damn." She narrowed her eyes and threw the words at him. "Why don't you go find a girl who will come to see you next time you get put away?"

The scar hardly moved when he spoke. "Things changed that much in three months?"

"They changed that much."

"You find somebody else to kind of help you forget about me?"

Now she laughed, once, with absolute bitterness. "Not one, baby, dozens! Didn't you see them all back there on the corner? They couldn't wait to get to me!"

Quietly: "All right. All right, be quiet." He put an arm around her and walked with her toward her apartment.

Later, when they had eaten and made love, she sat head in hands trying not to think while he talked at her. She paid no attention until he asked a question that she wanted to answer.

"Don't you ever wish for a decent-looking guy to come and get you out of that factory and out of this dump you live in . . . and away from me?"

"What would a decent-looking guy want with me?"

Instead of answering he said, "You still have that bottle of sleeping pills in your medicine cabinet?"

When she did not answer, he went to look. "Nonprescription now," he said when he came back. "What happened to the others?"

"I poured them down the toilet."

"Why?"

Again she did not answer.

After a moment, he said more gently, "When?"

"When I . . . when they put you in jail."

"And you acted like you didn't expect to see me again."

She shook her head. "I didn't."

"I don't want to die any more than you do."

She jumped and glanced at him. He knew better than to talk like that. He did it to hurt her. That was all.

She said, "I'd rather be dead than here picking up where we left off three months ago."

"Then why'd you throw out the pills?"

"So I would live. Without you."

He smiled. "And when did you decide you couldn't?"

She threw the heavy glass ashtray beside the bed. It flew wide of him, dented the wall behind him, and broke into three pieces.

He looked from the pieces to her. "You would have made your point better if you had tried to hit me."

She began to cry and she was not aware when the crying became screaming. "Get out of here! Leave me alone! *Leave me alone!*"

He didn't move.

Then her neighbor was pounding on the door to find out what all the noise was about. She calmed herself enough to open it, but while she was reassuring the woman that everything was all right, he came up behind her and stood there. She did not have to look around to know he was there. Still, she did not come near losing control until her neighbor said, "You must be lonesome over here by yourself. Why don't you come around to my apartment and talk for a while?"

It was as though her neighbor were playing a stupid childish joke on her. It should have been a joke. Somehow, she got rid of the woman without breaking down.

Then she turned and stared at the man—at the scar marring a face that had never been handsome. She shook her head, crying again but paying no attention to her tears. He seemed to know better than to touch her.

After a while she got her coat and started out the door.

"I'm going with you."

The look she gave him contained all the stored-up viciousness of the day. "Do whatever you want." She saw fear in his eyes for the first time.

"Where are you going?"

She said, "You didn't have to meet me on the street today. Or come to the door just now. You didn't have to talk about . . . "

"Jane, where are you going?"

There were few things she hated more than her own name. In all the time they had been together, he could not have used it more than twice. She slammed the door in his face.

"What am I that I could need you anyway?" She wished she had said the words to him but it didn't matter. It was just another of the things she didn't have the courage to do. Like accepting the loneliness or dying or . . .

She retraced her steps back to the liquor store. The boys had gone, but the wino was still there leaning against a telephone pole and holding a bag shaped by the bottle inside it.

"So you come back, huh?" He couldn't stand at a distance and talk. He had to put his face right up next to hers. It was an act of will for her not to vomit.

He thrust the bag at her. "You can have a little bit if you want. I got some more in my room. . . . "

She stared at the bottle for a moment, then almost snatched it from him. She drank without giving herself time to taste or think or gag. She had lived around drunks most of her life. She knew that if she could get enough down, nothing would matter.

She let the wino guide her toward the hotel. There was a scar-faced man coming toward them from down the block. She sucked another swallow from the bottle and waited for him to vanish.

Afterword

In the terrible little jobs that I used to get at factories, warehouses, food-processing plants, offices, and retail outlets, there always seemed to be at least one or two very odd people. Everyone knew about them. Sometimes they were actually on medication; sometimes not. But with or without medication, they had serious, noticeable problems.

I lived in terror of joining them. Those grindingly dull jobs, I thought, were capable of sending anyone up the wall. I suspect most of my coworkers thought I was already pretty strange. I spent my breaks writing, or I was tired and cranky from getting up early in the morning to write at home.

"Crossover" not only grew out of that time but was written during that time. It was written during the summer of 1970 at Clarion Science Fiction and Fantasy Writers' Workshop. When I went to Clarion I hadn't sold any of my stories. Then Robin Scott Wilson, at the time director of Clarion, bought "Crossover," and Harlan Ellison bought another of my stories. I was overjoyed. I thought I was on my way as a writer. No more failure and scut work. In fact, I had five more years of rejection slips and horrible little jobs ahead of me before I sold another word.

I didn't wind up hallucinating or turning to alcohol as the character in "Crossover" does, but I did keep noticing the company oddities everywhere I worked, and they went right on scaring me back to the typewriter whenever I strayed.

-Two Essays-

Positive Obsession

My mother read me bedtime stories until I was six years old. It was a sneak attack on her part. As soon as I really got to like the stories, she said, "Here's the book. Now you read." She didn't know what she was setting us both up for.

-2-

"I think," my mother said to me one day when I was ten, "that everyone has something that they can do better than they can do anything else. It's up to them to find out what that something is."

We were in the kitchen by the stove. She was pressing my hair while I sat bent over someone's cast-off notebook, writing. I had decided to write down some of the stories I'd been telling myself over the years. When I didn't have stories to read, I learned to make them up. Now I was learning to write them down.

-3-

I was shy, afraid of most people, most situations. I didn't stop to ask myself how things could hurt me, or even whether they could hurt me. I was just afraid.

I crept into my first bookstore full of vague fears. I had managed to save about five dollars, mostly in change. It was 1957. Five dollars was a lot of money for a ten-year-old. The public library had been my second home since I was six, and I owned a number of hand-me-down books. But now I wanted a new book—one I had chosen, one I could keep.

"Can kids come in here?" I asked the woman at the cash register once I was inside. I meant could Black kids come in. My mother, born in rural Louisiana and raised amid strict racial segregation, had warned me that I might not be welcome everywhere, even in California.

The cashier glanced at me. "Of course you can come in," she said. Then, as though it were an afterthought, she smiled. I relaxed.

The first book I bought described the characteristics of different breeds of horses. The second described stars and planets, asteroids, moons and comets.

-4-

My aunt and I were in her kitchen, talking. She was cooking something that smelled good, and I was sitting at her table, watching. Luxury. At home, my mother would have had me helping.

"I want to be a writer when I grow up," I said.

"Do you?" my aunt asked. "Well, that's nice, but you'll have to get a job, too."

"Writing will be my job," I said.

"You can write any time. It's a nice hobby. But you'll have to earn a living."

"As a writer."

"Don't be silly."

"I mean it."

"Honey . . . Negroes can't be writers."

"Why not?"

"They just can't."

"Yes, they can, too!"

I was most adamant when I didn't know what I was talking out. In all my thirteen years, I had never read a printed word that I knew to have been written by a Black person. My aunt was a grown woman. She knew more than I did. What if she were right?

-5-

Shyness is shit.

It isn't cute or feminine or appealing. It's torment, and it's shit.

I spent a lot of my childhood and adolescence staring at the ground. It's a wonder I didn't become a geologist. I whispered. People were always saying, "Speak up! We can't hear you."

I memorized required reports and poems for school, then cried my way out of having to recite. Some teachers condemned me for not studying. Some forgave me for not being very bright. Only a few saw my shyness.

"She's so backward," some of my relatives said.

"She's so nice and quiet," tactful friends of my mother said.

I believed I was ugly and stupid, clumsy, and socially hopeless. I also thought that everyone would notice these faults if I drew attention to myself. I wanted to disappear. Instead, I grew to be six feet tall. Boys in particular seemed to assume that I had done this growing deliberately and that I should be ridiculed for it as often as possible.

I hid out in a big pink notebook—one that would hold a whole ream of paper. I made myself a universe in it. There I could be a magic horse, a Martian, a telepath. . . . There I could be anywhere but here, any time but now, with any people but these.

-6-

My mother did day work. She had a habit of bringing home any books her employers threw out. She had been permitted only three years of school. Then she had been put to work. Oldest daughter. She believed passionately in books and education. She wanted me to have what she had been denied.

She wasn't sure which books I might be able to use, so she brought whatever she found in the trash. I had books yellow with age, books without covers, books written in, crayoned in, spilled on, cut, torn, even partly burned. I stacked them in wooden crates and second-hand bookcases and read them when I was ready for them. Some were years too advanced for me when I got them, but I grew into them.

-7-

An obsession, according to my old Random House dictionary, is "the domination of one's thoughts or feelings by a persistent idea, image, desire, etc." Obsession can be a useful tool if it's positive obsession. Using it is like aiming carefully in archery.

I took archery in high school because it wasn't a team sport. I liked some of the team sports, but in archery you did well or badly according to your own efforts. No one else to blame. I wanted to see what I could do. I learned to aim high. Aim above the target. Aim just *there!* Relax. Let go. If you aimed right, you hit the bull's-eye. I saw positive obsession as a way of aiming yourself, your life, at your chosen target. Decide what you want. Aim high. Go for it.

I wanted to sell a story. Before I knew how to type, I wanted to sell a story.

I pecked my stories out two fingered on the Remington portable typewriter my mother had bought me. I had begged for it when I was ten, and she had bought it.

"You'll spoil that child!" one of her friends told her. "What does she need with a typewriter at her age? It will soon be sitting in the closet with dust on it. All that money wasted!"

I asked my science teacher, Mr. Pfaff, to type one of my stories for me—type it the way it was supposed to be with no holes erased into the paper and no strike-overs. He did. He even corrected my terrible spelling and punctuation. To this day I'm amazed and grateful.

-8-

I had no idea how to submit a story for publication. I blundered through unhelpful library books on writing. Then I found a discarded copy of *The Writer*, a magazine I had never heard of. That copy sent me back to the library to look for more, and for other writers' magazines to see what I could learn from them. In very little time I'd found out how to submit a story, and my story was in the mail. A few weeks later I got my first rejection slip.

When I was older, I decided that getting a rejection slip was like being told your child was ugly. You got mad and didn't believe a word of it. Besides, look at all the really ugly literary children out there in the world being published and doing fine!

-9-

I spent my teens and much of my twenties collecting printed rejections. Early on, my mother lost $61.20—a reading fee charged by a so-called agent to look at one of my unpublishable stories. No one had told us that agents weren't supposed to get any money up front, weren't supposed to be paid until they sold your work. Then they were to take ten percent of whatever the work earned. Ignorance is expensive. That $61.20 was more money back then than my mother paid for a month's rent.

-10-

I badgered friends and acquaintances into reading my work, and they seemed to like it. Teachers read it and said kindly, unhelpful things. But there were no creative writing classes at my high school, and no useful criticism. At college (in California at that time, junior college was almost free), I took classes taught by an elderly woman who wrote children's stories. She was polite about the science fiction and fantasy that I kept handing in, but she finally asked in exasperation, "Can't you write anything normal?"

A schoolwide contest was held. All submissions had to be made anonymously. My short story won first prize. I was an eighteen-year-old freshman, and I won in spite of competition from older, more experienced people. Beautiful. The $15.00 prize was the first money my writing earned me.

-11-

After college I did office work for a while, then factory and warehouse work. My size and strength were advantages in factories and warehouses. And no one expected me to smile and pretend I was having a good time.

I got up at two or three in the morning and wrote. Then I went to work. I hated it, and I have no gift for suffering in silence. I muttered and complained and quit jobs and found new ones and collected more rejection slips. One day in disgust I threw them all away. Why keep such useless, painful things?

-12-

There seems to be an unwritten rule, hurtful and at odds with the realities of American culture. It says you aren't supposed to wonder whether as a Black person, a Black woman, you really might be inferior—not quite bright enough, not quite quick enough, not quite good enough to do the things you want to do. Though, of course, you do wonder. You're supposed to *know* you're as good as anyone. And if you don't know, you aren't supposed to admit it. If anyone near you admits it, you're supposed to reassure them quickly so they'll shut up. That sort of talk is embarrassing. Act tough and confident and don't talk about your doubts. If you never deal with them, you may never get rid of them, but no matter. Fake everyone out. Even yourself.

I couldn't fake myself out. I didn't talk much about my doubts. I wasn't fishing for hasty reassurances. But I did a lot of thinking—the same things over and over.

Who was I anyway? Why should anyone pay attention to what I had to say? Did I have anything to say? I was writing science fiction and fantasy, for God's sake. At that time nearly all professional science-fiction writers were white men. As much as I loved science fiction and fantasy, what was I doing?

Well, whatever it was, I couldn't stop. Positive obsession is about not being able to stop just because you're afraid and full of doubts. Positive obsession is dangerous. It's about not being able to stop at all.

-13-

I was twenty-three when, finally, I sold my first two short stories. I sold both to writer-editors who were teaching at Clarion, a science-fiction writers' workshop that I was attending. One story was eventually published. The other wasn't. I didn't sell another word for five years. Then, finally, I sold my first novel. Thank God no one told me selling would take so long—not that I would have believed it. I've sold eight novels since then. Last Christmas, I paid off the mortgage on my mother's house.

-14-

So, then, I write science fiction and fantasy for a living. As far as I know I'm still the only Black woman who does this. When I began to do a little public speaking, one of the questions I heard most often was, "What good is science fiction to Black people?" I was usually asked this by a Black person. I gave bits and pieces of answers that didn't satisfy me and that probably didn't satisfy my questioners. I resented the question. Why should I have to justify my profession to anyone?

But the answer to that was obvious. There was exactly one other Black science-fiction writer working successfully when I sold my first novel: Samuel R. Delany, Jr. Now there are four of us. Delany, Steven Barnes, Charles R. Saunders, and me. So few. Why? Lack of interest? Lack of confidence? A young Black woman once said to me, "I always wanted to write science fiction, but I didn't think there were any Black women doing it." Doubts show themselves in all sorts of ways. But still I'm asked, what good is science fiction to Black people?

What good is any form of literature to Black people?

What good is science fiction's thinking about the present, the future, and the past? What good is its tendency to warn or to consider alternative ways of thinking and doing? What good is its examination of the possible effects of science and technology, or social organization and political direction? At its best, science fiction stimulates imagination and creativity. It gets reader and writer off the beaten track, off the narrow, narrow footpath of what "everyone" is saying, doing, thinking—whoever "everyone" happens to be this year.

And what good is all this to Black people?

Afterword

This autobiographical article appeared originally in *Essence* magazine under the *Essence* title, "Birth of a Writer." I never liked the *Essence* title. My title was always "Positive Obsession."

I've often said that since my life was filled with reading, writing, and not much else, it was too dull to write about. I still feel that way. I'm glad I wrote this piece, but I didn't enjoy writing it. I have no doubt at all that the best and the most interesting part of me is my fiction.

Furor Scribendi

Writing for publication may be both the easiest and the hardest thing you'll ever do. Learning the rules—if they can be called rules—is the easy part. Following them, turning them into regular habits, is an ongoing struggle. Here are the rules:

1. Read. Read about the art, the craft, and the business of writing. Read the kind of work you'd like to write. Read good literature and bad, fiction and fact. Read every day and learn from what you read. If you commute to work or if you spend part of your day doing relatively mindless work, listen to book tapes. If your library doesn't have a good supply of complete books on audio tape, companies like Recorded Books, Books on Tape, Brilliance Corporation, and the Literate Ear will rent or sell you a wide selection of such books for your pleasure and continuing education. These provide a painless way to ponder use of language, the sounds of words, conflict, characterization, plotting, and the multitudes of ideas you can find in history, biography, medicine, the sciences, etc.

2. Take classes and go to writers' workshops. Writing is communication. You need other people to let you know whether you're communicating what you think you are and whether you're doing it in ways that are not only accessible and entertaining, but as compelling as you can make them. In

other words, you need to know that you're telling a good story. You want to be the writer who keeps readers up late at night, not the one who drives them off to watch television. Workshops and classes are rented readers—rented audiences—for your work. Learn from the comments, questions, and suggestions of both the teacher and the class. These relative strangers are more likely to tell you the truth about your work than are your friends and family who may not want to hurt or offend you. One tiresome truth they might tell you, for instance, is that you need to take a grammar class. If they say this, listen. Take the class. Vocabulary and grammar are your primary tools. They're most effectively used, even most effectively abused, by people who understand them. No computer program, no friend or employee can take the place of a sound knowledge of your tools.

3. Write. Write every day. Write whether you feel like writing or not. Choose a time of day. Perhaps you can get up an hour earlier, stay up an hour later, give up an hour of recreation, or even give up your lunch hour. If you can't think of anything in your chosen genre, keep a journal. You should be keeping one anyway. Journal writing helps you to be more observant of your world, and a journal is a good place to store story ideas for later projects.

4. Revise your writing until it's as good as you can make it. All the reading, the writing, and the classes should help you do this. Check your writing, your research (never neglect your research), and the physical appearance of your manuscript. Let nothing substandard slip through. If you notice something that needs fixing, fix it, no excuses. There will be plenty that's wrong that you won't catch. Don't make the mistake of ignor-

ing flaws that are obvious to you. The moment you find yourself saying, "This doesn't matter. It's good enough." Stop. Go back. Fix the flaw. Make a habit of doing your best.

5. Submit your work for publication. First research the markets that interest you. Seek out and study the books or magazines of publishers to whom you want to sell. Then submit your work. If the idea of doing this scares you, fine. Go ahead and be afraid. But send your work out anyway. If it's rejected, send it out again, and again. Rejections are painful, but inevitable. They're every writer's rite of passage. Don't give up on a piece of work that you can't sell. You may be able to sell it later to new publications or to new editors of old publications. At worst, you should be able to learn from your rejected work. You may even be able to use all or part of it in a new work. One way or another, writers can use, or at least learn from, everything.

6. Here are some potential impediments for you to forget about:

First forget *inspiration.* Habit is more dependable. Habit will sustain you whether you're inspired or not. Habit will help you finish and polish your stories. Inspiration won't. Habit is persistence in practice.

Forget *talent.* If you have it, fine. Use it. If you don't have it, it doesn't matter. As habit is more dependable than inspiration, continued learning is more dependable than talent. Never let pride or laziness prevent you from learning, improving your work, changing its direction when necessary. Persistence is essential to any writer—the persistence to finish your work, to keep writing in spite of rejection, to keep reading, studying, submitting work for sale. But stubbornness, the refusal to change unproductive behavior or to revise unsalable work can be lethal to your writing hopes.

Finally, don't worry about imagination. You have all the imagination you need, and all the reading, journal writing, and learning you will be doing will stimulate it. Play with your ideas. Have fun with them. Don't worry about being silly or outrageous or wrong. So much of writing is fun. It's first letting your interests and your imagination take you anywhere at all. Once you're able to do that, you'll have more ideas than you can use. Then the real work of fashioning them into a story begins. Stay with it.

Persist.

Afterword

I wrote this brief essay for the *Writers of the Future* anthology series (*L. Ron Hubbard Presents Writers of the Future IX*). This series showcases the work of new writers, and my essay is a compact version of a talk that I've given to groups of new writers.

The last word of the essay is its most important word. Writing is difficult. You do it all alone without encouragement and without any certainty that you'll ever be published or paid or even that you'll be able to finish the particular work you've begun. It isn't easy to persist amid all that. That's why I've called this mild little essay "Furor Scribendi"—"A Rage for Writing." "Rage," "Positive Obsession," "burning need to write" . . . Call it anything you like; it's a useful emotion.

Sometimes when I'm interviewed, the interviewer either compliments me on my "talent," my "gift," or asks me how I discovered it. (I don't know, maybe it was supposed to be lying in my closet or on the street somewhere, waiting to be discovered.) I used to struggle to answer this politely, to explain that I didn't believe much in writing talent. People who want to write either do it or they don't. At last I began to say that my most important talent—or habit—was *persistence*. Without it, I would have given up writing long before I finished my first novel. It's amazing what we can do if we simply refuse to give up.

I suspect that this is the most important thing I've said in all my interviews and talks as well as in this book. It's a truth that applies to more than writing. It applies to anything that is important, but difficult, important, but frightening. We're all capable of climbing so much higher than we usually permit ourselves to suppose.

The word, again, is "persist"!

-New Stories-

Amnesty

The stranger-Community, globular, easily twelve feet high and wide glided down into the vast, dimly lit food production hall of Translator Noah Cannon's employer. The stranger was incongruously quick and graceful, keeping to the paths, never once brushing against the raised beds of fragile, edible fungi. It looked, Noah thought, a little like a great, black, moss-enshrouded bush with such a canopy of irregularly-shaped leaves, shaggy mosses, and twisted vines that no light showed through it. It had a few thick, naked branches growing out, away from the main body, breaking the symmetry and making the Community look in serious need of pruning.

The moment Noah saw it and saw her employer, a somewhat smaller, better-maintained-looking dense, black bush, back away from her, she knew she would be offered the new job assignment she had been asking for.

The stranger-Community settled, flattening itself at bottom, allowing its organisms of mobility to migrate upward and take their rest. The stranger-Community focused its attention on Noah, electricity flaring and zigzagging, making a visible display within the dark vastness of its body. She knew that the electrical display was speech, although she could not read what was said. The Communities spoke in this way between themselves and within themselves, but the light they produced moved far too quickly for her to even begin to learn the language.

The fact that she saw the display, though, meant that the communications entities of the stranger-Community were addressing her. Communities used their momentarily inactive organisms to shield communication from anyone outside themselves who was not being addressed.

She glanced at her employer and saw that its attention was focused away from her. It had no noticeable eyes, but its entities of vision served it very well whether she could see them or not. It had drawn itself together, made itself look more like a spiny stone than a bush. Communities did this when they wished to offer others privacy or simply disassociate themselves from the business being transacted. Her employer had warned her that the job that would be offered to her would be unpleasant not only because of the usual hostility of the human beings she would face, but because the subcontractor for whom she would be working would be difficult. The subcontractor had had little contact with human beings. Its vocabulary in the painfully created common language that enabled humans and the Communities to speak to one another was, at best, rudimentary, as was its understanding of human abilities and limitations. Translation: by accident or by intent, the subcontractor would probably hurt her. Her employer had told her that she did not have to take this job, that it would support her if she chose not to work for this subcontractor. It did not altogether approve of her decision to try for the job anyway. Now it's deliberate inattention had more to do with disassociation than with courtesy or privacy. "You're on your own," its posture said, and she smiled. She could never have worked for it if it had not been able to stand aside and let her make her own decisions. Yet it did not go about its business and leave her alone with the stranger. It waited.

And here was the subcontractor signaling her with lightning.

Obediently, she went to it, stood close to it so that the tips of what looked like moss-covered outer twigs and branches touched her bare skin. She wore only shorts and a halter top. The Communities would have preferred her to be naked, and for the long years of her captivity, she had had no choice. She had been naked. Now she was no longer a captive, and she insisted on wearing at least the basics. Her employer had come to accept this and now refused to lend her to subcontractors who would refuse her the right to wear clothing.

This subcontractor enfolded her immediately, drawing her upward and in among its many selves, first hauling her up with its various organisms of manipulation, then grasping her securely with what appeared to be moss. The Communities were not plants, but it was easiest to think of them in those terms since most of the time, most of them looked so plantlike.

Enfolded within the Community, she couldn't see at all. She closed her eyes to avoid the distraction of trying to see or imagining that she saw. She felt herself surrounded by what felt like long, dry fibers, fronds, rounded fruits of various sizes, and other things that produced less identifiable sensations. She was at once touched, stroked, messaged, compressed in the strangely comfortable, peaceful way that she had come to look forward to whenever she was employed. She was turned and handled as though she weighed nothing. In fact, after a few moments, she felt weightless. She had lost all sense of direction, yet she felt totally secure, clasped by entities that had nothing resembling human limbs. Why this was pleasurable, she never understood, but for twelve years of captivity, it had been her only dependable comfort. It had happened often enough to enable her to endure everything else that was done to her.

Fortunately, the Communities also found it comforting—even more than she did.

After a while, she felt the particular rhythm of quick warning pressures across her back. The Communities liked the broad expanse of skin that the human back offered.

She made a beckoning motion with her right hand to let the Community know that she was paying attention.

There are six recruits, it signaled with pressures against her back. You will teach them.

I will, she signed, using her hands and arms only. The Communities liked her signs to be small, confined gestures when she was enfolded and large, sweeping hand, arm, and whole-body efforts when she was outside and not being touched. She had wondered at first if this was because they couldn't see very well. Now she knew that they could see far better than she could—could see over great distances with specialized entities of vision, could see most bacteria and some viruses, and see colors from ultraviolet through infrared.

In fact the reason that they preferred large gestures when she was out of contact and unlikely to hit or kick anyone was because they liked to watch her move. It was that simple, that odd. In fact, the Communities had developed a real liking for human dance performances and for some human sports events—especially individual performances in gymnastics and ice skating.

The recruits are disturbed, the sub-contractor said. They may be dangerous to one another. Calm them.

I will try, Noah said. I will answer their questions and reassure them that they have nothing to fear. Privately, she suspected that hate might be a more prevalent emotion than fear, but if the subcontractor didn't know that, she wouldn't tell it.

Calm them. The subcontractor repeated. And she knew then that it meant, literally, "Change them from disturbed people to calm, willing workers." The Communities could change one another just by exchanging a few of their individual entities—as long as both exchanging communities were willing. Too many of them assumed that human beings should be able to do something like this too, and that if they wouldn't, they were just being stubborn.

Noah repeated, I will answer their questions and reassure them that they have nothing to fear. That's all I can do.

Will they be calm?

She drew a deep breath, knowing that she was about to be hurt—twisted or torn, broken or stunned. Many Communities punished refusal to obey orders—as they saw it—less harshly than they punished what they saw as lying. In fact, the punishments were left over from the years when human beings were captives of uncertain ability, intellect, and perception. People were not supposed to be punished any longer, but of course they were. Now, Noah thought it was best to get whatever punishment there might be out of the way at once. She could not escape. She signed stolidly, Some of them may believe what I tell them and be calm. Others will need time and experience to calm them.

She was, at once, held more tightly, almost painfully—"held hard" as the Communities called it, held so that she could not move even her arms, could not harm any members of the Community by thrashing about in pain. Just before she might have been injured by the squeezing alone, it stopped.

She was hit with a sudden electrical shock that convulsed

her. It drove the breath out of her in a hoarse scream. It made her see flashes of light even with her eyes tightly closed. It stimulated her muscles into abrupt, agonizing contortions.

Calm them, the Community insisted once again.

She could not answer at first. It took her a moment to get her now sore and shaking body under control and to understand what was being said to her. It took her a moment more to be able to flex her hands and arms, now free again, and finally to shape an answer—the only possible answer in spite of what it might cost.

I will answer their questions and reassure them that they have nothing to fear.

She was held hard for several seconds more, and knew that she might be given another shock. After a while, though, there were several flashes of light that she saw out of the corner of her eye, but that did not seem to have anything to do with her. Then without any more communication, Noah was passed into the care of her employer, and the subcontractor was gone.

She saw nothing as she was passed from darkness to darkness. There was nothing to hear but the usual rustle of Communities moving about. There was no change of scent, or if there was, her nose was not sensitive enough to detect it. Yet somehow, she had learned to know her employer's touch. She relaxed in relief.

Are you injured? her employer signed.

No, she answered. Just aching joints and other sore places. Did I get the job?

Of course you did. You must tell me if that subcontractor tries to coerce you again. It knows better. I've told it that if it injures you, I will never allow you to work for it again.

Thank you.

There was a moment of stillness. Then the employer stroked her, calming her and pleasing itselves. You insist on taking these jobs, but you can't use them to make the changes you want to make. You know that. You cannot change your people or mine.

I can, a little, she signed. Community by Community, human by human. I would work faster if I could.

And so you let subcontractors abuse you. You try to help your own people to see new possibilities and understand changes that have already happened but most of them won't listen and they hate you.

I want to make them think. I want to tell them what human governments won't tell them. I want to vote for peace between your people and mine by telling the truth. I don't know whether my efforts will do any good, in the long run, but I have to try.

Let yourself heal. Rest enfolded until the subcontractor returns for you.

Noah sighed, content, within another moment of stillness. Thank you for helping me, even though you don't believe.

I would like to believe. But you can't succeed. Right now groups of your people are looking for ways to destroy us.

Noah winced. I know. Can you stop them without killing them?

Her employer shifted her. Stroked her. Probably not, it signed. Not again.

• • •

"Translator," Michelle Ota began as the applicants trailed into the meeting room, "do these . . . these things . . . actually understand that we're intelligent?"

She followed Noah into the meeting room, waited to see where Noah would sit, and sat next to her. Noah noticed that Michelle Ota was one of only two of the six applicants who was willing to sit near her even for this informal question-and-answer session. Noah had information that they needed. She was doing a job some of them might wind up doing someday, and yet that job—translator and personnel officer for the Communities—and the fact that she could do it was their reason for distrusting her. The second person who wanted to sit near her was Sorrel Trent. She was interested in alien spirituality—whatever that might be.

The four remaining job candidates choose to leave empty seats between themselves and Noah.

"Of course the Communities know we're intelligent," Noah said.

"I mean I know you work for them," Michelle Ota glanced at her, hesitated then went on. "I want to work for them too. Because at least they're hiring. Almost nobody else is. But what do they think of us?"

"They'll be offering some of you contracts soon," Noah said. "They wouldn't waste time doing that if they'd mistaken you for cattle." She relaxed back into her chair, watching some of the six other people in the room get water, fruit or nuts from the sideboards. The food was good and clean and free to them whether or not they were hired. It was also, she knew, the first food most of them had had that day. Food was expensive and in these depressed times, most people were lucky to eat once a day. It pleased her to see them enjoying it. She was the one who had insisted there be food in the meeting rooms for the question and answer sessions.

She herself was enjoying the rare comfort of wearing shoes, long black cotton pants, and a colorful flowing tunic. And there was furniture designed for the human body—an upholstered armchair with a high back and a table she could eat from or rest her arms on. She had no such furniture in her quarters within the Mojave Bubble. She suspected that she could have at least the furniture now, if she asked her employer for it, but she had not asked, would not ask. Human things were for human places.

"But what does a contract mean to things that come from another star system?" Michelle Ota demanded.

Rune Johnsen spoke up. "Yes, it's interesting how quickly these beings have taken up local, terrestrial ways when it suits them. Translator, do you truly believe they will consider themselves bound by anything they sign? Although without hands, God knows how they manage to sign anything."

"They will consider both themselves and you bound by it if both they and you sign it," Noah said. "And, yes, they can make highly individual marks that serve as signatures. They spent a great deal of their time and wealth in this country with translators, lawyers, and politicians, working things out so that each Community was counted as a legal 'person,' whose individual mark would be accepted. And for twenty years since then, they've honored their contracts."

Rune Johnsen shook his blond head. "In all, they've been on earth longer than I've been alive, and yet it feels wrong that they're here. It feels wrong that they exist. I don't even hate them, and still it feels wrong. I suppose that's because we've been displaced again from the center of the universe. We human beings, I mean. Down through history, in myth and even in science, we've kept putting ourselves in the center, and then being evicted."

Noah smiled, surprised and pleased. "I noticed the same thing. Now we find ourselves in a kind of sibling rivalry with the Communities. There is other intelligent life. The universe has other children. We knew it, but until they arrived here, we could pretend otherwise."

"That's crap!" another woman said. Thera Collier, her name was, a big, angry, red-haired young woman. "The weeds came here uninvited, stole our land, and kidnapped our people," She had been eating an apple. She slammed it down hard on the table, crushing what was left of it, spattering juice. "That's what we need to remember. That's what we need to do something about."

"Do what?" Another woman asked. "We're here to get jobs, not fight."

Noah searched her memory for the new speaker's name and found it. Piedad Ruiz—a small, brown woman who spoke English clearly, but with a strong Spanish accent. She looked with her bruised face and arms as though she had taken a fairly serious beating recently, but when Noah had asked her about it before the group came into the meeting room, she held her head up and said she was fine and it was nothing. Probably someone had not wanted her to apply for work at the bubble. Considering the rumors that were sometimes spread about the Communities and why they hired human beings, that was not surprising.

"What have the aliens told you about their coming here, Translator," Rune Johnsen asked. He was, Noah remembered from her reading of the short biography that had been given to her with his job application, the son of a small businessman whose clothing store had not survived the depression brought about by the arrival of the Communities. He wanted to look after his parents and he wanted to get married. Ironically, the answer to both those problems seemed to be to go to work for the Communities for a while. "You're old enough to remember the things they did when they arrived," he said. "What did they tell you about why they abducted people, killed people. . . ."

"They abducted me," Noah admitted.

That silenced the room for several seconds. Each of the six potential recruits stared at her, perhaps wondering or pitying, judging or worrying, perhaps even recoiling in horror, suspicion, or disgust. She had received all these reactions from recruits and from others who knew her history. People had never been able to be neutral about abductees. Noah tended to use her history as a way to start questions, accusations, and perhaps thought.

"Noah Cannon," Rune Johnsen said, proving that he had at least been listening when she introduced herself. "I thought that name sounded familiar. You were part of the second wave of abductions. I remember seeing your name on the lists of abductees. I noticed it because you were listed as female. I had never run across a woman named Noah before."

"So they kidnapped you, and now you work for them?" This was James Hunter Adio, a tall, lean, angry-looking young black man. Noah was black herself and yet James Adio had apparently decided the moment they met that he didn't like her. Now he looked not only angry, but disgusted.

"I was eleven when I was taken," Noah said. She looked at Rune Johnsen. "You're right. I was part of the second wave."

"So what, then, they experimented on you?" James Adio asked.

Noah met his gaze. "They did, yes. The people of the first wave suffered the most. The Communities didn't know anything about us. They killed some of us with experiments and dietary deficiency diseases and they poisoned others. By the time they snatched me, they at least knew enough not to kill me by accident."

"And what? You forgive them for what they did do?"

"Are you angry with me, Mr. Adio, or are you angry in my behalf?"

"I'm angry because I have to be here!" he said. He stood up and paced around the table—all the way around twice before he would sit down again. "I'm angry that these things, these weeds can invade us, wreck our economies, send the whole world into a depression just by showing up. They do whatever they want to us, and instead of killing them, all I can do is ask them for a job!" And he needed the job badly. Noah had read the information collected about him when he first applied to work for the Communities. At twenty, James Adio was the oldest of seven children, and the only one who had reached adulthood so far. He needed a job to help his younger brothers and sisters survive. Yet Noah suspected that he would hate the aliens almost as much if they hired him as if they turned him down.

"How can you work for them?" Piedad Ruiz whispered to Noah. "They hurt you. Don't you hate them? I think I'd hate them if it were me."

"They wanted to understand us and communicate with us," Noah said. "They wanted to know how we got along with one another and they needed to know how much we could bear of what was normal for them."

"Is that what they told you?" Thera Collier demanded. With one hand, she swept her smashed apple off the table onto the floor, and then glared at Noah as though wishing she could sweep her away too. Watching her, Noah realized that Thera

Collier was a very frightened woman. Well, they were all frightened, but Thera's fear made her lash out at people.

"The Communities did tell me that," Noah admitted, "but not until some of them and some of us, the surviving captives, had managed to put together a code—the beginnings of a language—that got communication started. Back when they captured me, they couldn't tell me anything."

Thera snorted. "Right. They can figure out how to cross light years of space, but they can't figure out how to talk to us without torturing us first!"

Noah allowed herself a moment of irritation. "You weren't there, Ms. Collier. It happened before you were born. And it happened to me, not to you." And it hadn't happened to anyone in Thera Collier's family either. Noah had checked. None of these people were relatives of abductees. It was important to know that since relatives sometimes tried to take revenge on translators when they realized they weren't going to be able to hurt the Communities.

"It happened to a lot of people," Thera Collier said. "And it shouldn't have happened to anyone."

Noah shrugged.

"Don't you hate them for what they did to you?" Piedad whispered. Whispering seemed to be her normal way of speaking.

"I don't," Noah said. "I did once, especially when they were beginning to understand us a little, and yet went right on putting us through hell. They were like human scientists experimenting with lab animals—not cruel, but very thorough."

"Animals again," Michelle Ota said. "You said they—"

"Then," Noah told her. "Not now."

"Why do you defend them?" Thera demanded. "They

invaded our world. They tortured our people. They do whatever they please, and we aren't even sure what they look like."

Rune Johnsen spoke up, to Noah's relief. "What do they look like, Translator? You've seen them close up."

Noah almost smiled. What did the Communities look like. That was usually the first question asked in a group like this. People tended to assume, no matter what they had seen or heard from media sources, that each Community was actually an individual being shaped like a big bush or tree or, more likely, that the being was wearing shrubbery as clothing or as a disguise.

"They're not like anything that any of us have ever known," she told them. "I've heard them compared to sea urchins—completely wrong. I've also heard they were like swarms of bees or wasps—also wrong, but closer. I think of them as what I usually call them—Communities. Each Community contains several hundred individuals—an intelligent multitude. But that's wrong too, really. The individuals can't really survive independently, but they can leave one community and move temporarily or permanently to another. They are products of a completely different evolution. When I look at them, I see what you've all seen: outer branches and then darkness. Flashes of light and movement within. Do you want to hear more?"

They nodded, sat forward attentively except for James Adio who leaned back with an expression of contempt on his dark, smooth young face.

"The substance of the things that look like branches and the things that look like leaves and mosses and vines is alive and made up of individuals. It only looks like a plant of some sort. The various entities that we can reach from the outside feel dry, and usually smooth. One normal-sized Community might fill half of this room, but only weigh about six to eight hundred pounds. They aren't solid, of course, and within them, there are entities that I've never seen. Being enveloped by a community is like being held in a sort of . . . comfortable strait jacket, if you can imagine such a thing. You can't move much. You can't move at all unless the Community permits it. You can't see anything. There's no smell. Somehow, though, after the first time, it isn't frightening. It's peaceful and pleasant. I don't know why it should be, but it is."

"Hypnosis," James Adio said at once. "Or drugs!"

"Definitely not," Noah said. At least this was something she could be sure of. "That was one of the hardest parts of being a captive of the Communities. Until they got to know us, they didn't have anything like hypnosis or mood-altering drugs. They didn't even have the concept."

Rune Johnsen turned to frown at her. "What concept?"

"Altered consciousness. They don't even go unconscious unless they're sick or injured, and a whole Community never goes unconscious even though several of its entities might. As a result, Communities can't really be said to sleep—although at long last, they've accepted the reality that we have to sleep. Inadvertently, we've introduced them to something brand new."

"Will they let us bring medicine in?" Michelle Ota asked suddenly. "I have allergies and I really need my medicine."

"They will allow certain medicines. If you're offered a contract, you'll have to write in the drugs you'll need. They will either allow you to have the drugs or you won't be hired. If what you need is allowed, you'll be permitted to order it from outside. The Communities will check to see that it is what it's supposed to be, but other than that, they won't bother you about it. Medicine's just about all you'll have to spend money on while you're inside. Room and board are part of the agreement, of course, and you won't be allowed to leave your employers until your contract is up."

"What if we get sick or have an accident?" Piedad demanded. "What if we need some medicine that isn't in the contract."

"Medical emergencies are covered by the contract," Noah said.

Thera slapped her palms down against the table and said loudly, "Screw all that!" She got the attention she wanted. Everyone turned to look at her. "I want to know more about you, and the weeds, Translator. In particular, I want to know why you're still here, working for things that probably put you through hell. Part of that no drug thing was no anesthetic when they hurt you, right?"

Noah sat still for a moment, remembering, yet not wanting to remember. "Yes," she said at last, "except that most of the time, the people actually hurting me were other human beings. The aliens used to lock groups of two or more of us up together for days or weeks to see what would happen. This was usually not too bad. Sometimes, though, it went wrong. Some of us went out of our minds. Hell, all of us went out of our minds at one time or another. But some of us were more likely than others to be violent. Then there were those of us who would have been thugs even without the Communities' help. They were quick enough to take advantage of any chance to exercise a little power, get a little pleasure by making another person suffer. And some of us just stopped caring, stopped fighting, sometimes even stopped eating. The pregnancies and several of the killings came from those cell-mate experiments. We called them that.

"It was almost easier when the aliens just made us solve puzzles to get food or when they put things in our food that made us sick or when they enfolded us and introduced some nearly lethal substance into our bodies. The first captives got most of that, poor people. And some of them had developed a phobic terror of being enfolded. They were lucky if that was all they developed."

"My God," Thera said, shaking her head in disgust. After a while, she asked, "What happened to the babies? You said some people got pregnant."

"The Communities don't reproduce the way we do. It didn't seem to occur to them for a long time to take it easy on the pregnant women. Because of that, most women who got pregnant miscarried. Some had still births. Four of the women in the group that I was usually caged with between experiments died in childbirth. None of us knew how to help them." That was another memory she wanted to turn away from.

"There were a few live births, and of those, a few babies survived infancy, even though their mothers couldn't protect them from the worst and the craziest of our own people or from the Communities who were . . . curious about them. In all thirty-seven of the world's bubbles, fewer than a hundred such children survived. Most of those have grown up to be reasonably sane adults. Some live outside in secret, and some will never leave the bubbles. Their choice. A few of them are becoming the best of the next generation of translators."

Rune Johnsen made a wordless sound of interest. "I've read about such children," he said.

"We tried to find some of them," Sorrel Trent said, speaking up for the first time. "Our leader teaches that they're the ones who will show us the way. They're so important, and yet our stupid government keeps them hidden!" She sounded both frustrated and angry.

"The governments of this world have a great deal to answer for," Noah said. "In some countries, the children won't come out of the bubbles because word has gotten back to them about what's happened to those who have come out. Word about disappearances, imprisonment, torture, death. Our government seems not to be doing that sort of thing any more. Not to the children, anyway. It's given them new identities to hide them from groups who want to worship them or kill them or set them apart. I've checked on some of them myself. They're all right, and they want to be let alone."

"My group doesn't want to hurt them," Sorrel Trent said. "We want to honor them and help them fulfill their true destiny."

Noah turned away from the woman, her mind filled with caustic, unprofessional things best not said. "So the children at least, are able to have a little peace," she did say.

"Is one of them yours?" Thera asked, her voice uncharacteristically soft. "Do you have children?"

Noah stared at her, then leaned her head against the chair back again. "I got pregnant when I was fifteen and again when I was seventeen. Miscarriages both times, thank God."

"It was . . . rape?" Rune Johnsen asked.

"Of course it was rape! Can you actually believe I'd want to give the Communities another human infant to study?" She stopped and took a deep breath. After a moment, she said, "Some of the deaths were women killed for resisting rape. Some of the deaths were rapists. Do you remember an old experiment in which too many rats are caged together and they begin to kill one another."

"But you weren't rats," Thera said. "You were intelligent. You could see what the weeds were doing to you. You didn't have to—"

Noah cut her off. "I didn't have to what?"

Thera backpedaled. "I didn't mean you personally. I just mean human beings ought to be able to behave better than a bunch of rats."

"Many did. Some did not."

"And in spite of all that, you work for the aliens. You forgive them because they didn't know what they were doing. Is that it?"

"They're here," Noah said flatly.

"They're here until we find a way to drive them away!"

"They're here to stay," Noah said more softly. "There's no 'away' for them—not for several generations anyway. Their ship was a one-way transport. They've settled here and they'll fight to keep the various desert locations they've chosen for their bubbles. If they do decide to fight, we won't survive. They might be destroyed too, but chances are, they would send their young deep into the ground for a few centuries. When they came up, this would be their world. We would be gone." She looked at each member of the group. "They're here," she said for the third time. "I'm one of maybe thirty people in this country who can talk to them. Where else would I be but here at a bubble, trying to help the two species understand and accept one another before one of them does something fatal?"

Thera was relentless. "But do you forgive them for what they've done?"

Noah shook her head. "I don't forgive them," she said. "They haven't asked for my forgiveness and I wouldn't know how to give it if they did. And that doesn't matter. It doesn't stop me from doing my job. It doesn't stop them from employing me."

James Adio said, "If they're as dangerous as you believe, you ought to be working with the government, trying to find a way to kill them. Like you said, you know more about them than the rest of us."

"Are you here to kill them, Mr. Adio?" Noah asked quietly.

He let his shoulders slump. "I'm here to work for them, lady. I'm poor. I don't have all kinds of special knowledge that only thirty people in the whole country have. I just need a job."

She nodded as though he had simply been conveying information, as though his words had not carried heavy loads of bitterness, anger, and humiliation. "You can make money here." She said. "I'm wealthy myself. I'm putting half a dozen nieces and nephews through college. My relatives eat three meals a day and live in comfortable homes. Why shouldn't yours?"

"Thirty pieces of silver," he muttered.

Noah gave him a tired smile. "Not for me," she said. "My parents seemed to have a completely different role in mind for me when they named me."

Rune Johnsen smiled but James Adio only stared at her with open dislike. Noah let her face settle into its more familiar solemnity. "Let me tell you all about my experience working with the government to get the better of the Communities," she said. "You should hear about it whether or not you choose to believe." She paused, gathered her thoughts.

• • •

"I was held here in the Mojave Bubble from my eleventh year through my twenty-third," she began. "Of course, none of my family or friends knew where I was or whether I was alive. I just disappeared like a lot of other people. In my case, I disappeared from my own bedroom in my parents' house in Victorville late one night. Years later when the Communities could talk to us, when they understood more of what they'd done to us, they asked a group of us whether we would stay with them voluntarily or whether we wanted to leave. I thought it might have been just another of their tests, but when I asked to go, they agreed.

"In fact, I was the first to ask to go. The group I was with then was made up of people taken in childhood—sometimes early childhood. Some of them were afraid to go out. They had no memory of any home but the Mojave Bubble. But I remembered my family. I wanted to see them again. I wanted to go out and not be confined to a small area in a bubble. I wanted to be free.

"But when the Communities let me go, they didn't take me back to Victorville. They just opened the bubble late one night near one of the shanty towns that had grown up around its perimeters. The shanty towns were wilder and cruder back then. They were made up of people who were worshipping the Communities or plotting to wipe them out or hoping to steal some fragment of valuable technology from them—that kind of thing. And some of the squatters there were undercover cops of one kind or another. The ones who grabbed me said they were FBI, but I think now that they might have been bounty hunters. In those days, there was a bounty on anyone or anything that came out of the bubbles, and it was my bad luck to be the first person to be seen coming out of the Mojave Bubble.

"Anyone coming out might know valuable technological secrets, or might be hypnotized saboteurs or disguised alien spies—any damned thing. I was handed over to the military which locked me up, questioned me relentlessly, accused me of everything from espionage to murder, from terrorism to treason. I was sampled and tested in every way they could think of. They convinced themselves that I was a valuable catch, that I had been collaborating with our "nonhuman enemies." Therefore, I represented a great opportunity to find a way to get at them—at the Communities.

"Everything I knew, they found out. It wasn't as though I was ever trying to hold anything back from them. The problem was, I couldn't tell them the kind of thing they wanted to know. Of course the Communities hadn't explained to me the workings of their technology. Why would they? I didn't know much about their physiology either, but I told what I did know—told it over and over again with my jailers trying to catch me in lies. And as for the Communities' psychology, I could only say what had been done to me and what I'd seen done to others. And because my jailers didn't see that as very useful, they decided I was being uncooperative, and that I had something to hide."

Noah shook her head. "The only difference between the way they treated me and the way the aliens treated me during the early years of my captivity was that the so-called human beings knew when they were hurting me. They questioned me day and night, threatened me, drugged me, all in an effort to get me to give them information I didn't have. They'd keep me awake for days on end, keep me awake until I couldn't think, couldn't tell what was real and what wasn't. They couldn't get at the aliens, but they had me. When they weren't questioning me, they kept me locked up, alone, isolated from everyone but them."

Noah looked around the room. "All this because they knew—knew absolutely—that a captive who survived twelve years of captivity and who is then freed must be a traitor of some kind, willing or unwilling, knowing or unknowing. They x-rayed me, scanned me in every possible way, and when they found nothing unusual, it only made them angrier, made them hate me more. I was, somehow, making fools of them. They knew it! And I wasn't going to get away with it.

"I gave up. I decided that they were never going to stop, that they would eventually kill me anyway, and until they did, I would never know any peace."

She paused remembering humiliation, fear, hopelessness, exhaustion, bitterness, sickness, pain. . . . They had never beaten her badly—just struck a few blows now and then for emphasis and intimidation. And sometimes she was grabbed, shaken, and shoved, amid ongoing accusations, speculations, and threats. Now and then, an interrogator, knocked her to the floor, then ordered her back to her chair. They did nothing that they thought might seriously injure or kill her. But it went on and on and on. Sometimes one of them pretended to be nice to her, courted her in a sense, tried to seduce her into telling secrets she did not know. . . .

"I gave up," she repeated. "I don't know how long I'd been there when that happened. I never saw the sky or sunlight so I lost all track of time. I just regained consciousness after a long session, found that I was in my cell alone, and decided to kill myself. I had been thinking about it off and on when I could think, and suddenly, I knew I would do it. Nothing else would make them stop. So I did do it. I hanged myself."

Piedad Ruiz made a wordless sound of distress, then stared downward at the table when people looked at her.

"You tried to kill yourself?" Rune Johnsen asked. "Did you do that when you were with the . . . the Communities?"

Noah shook her head. "I never did." She paused. "It mattered more than I know how to tell you that this time my tormentors were my own people. They were human. They spoke my language. They knew all that I knew about pain and humiliation and fear and despair. They knew what they were doing to me, and yet it never occurred to them not to do it." She thought for a moment, remembering. "Some captives of the Communities did kill themselves. And the Communities didn't care. If you wanted to die and managed to hurt yourself badly enough, you'd die. They'd watch."

But if you didn't choose to die, there was the perverse security and peace of being enfolded. There was, somehow, the pleasure of being enfolded. It happened often when captives were not being tested in some way. It happened because the entities of the Communities discovered that it pleased and comforted them too, and they didn't understand why any more than she did. The first enfoldings happened because they were convenient ways of restraining, examining, and, unhappily, poisoning human captives. It wasn't long, though, before unoccupied humans were being enfolded just for the pleasure the act gave to an unoccupied Community. Communities did not understand at first that their captives could also take pleasure in the act. Human children like Noah learned quickly how to approach a Community and touch its outer branches to ask to be enfolded, although adult human captives had tried to prevent the practice, and to punish it when they could not prevent it. Noah had had to grow up to even begin to understand why adult captives sometimes beat children for daring to ask alien captors for comfort.

Noah had met her current employer before she turned twelve. It was one of the Communities who never injured her, one who had worked with her and with others to begin to assemble a language that both species could use.

She sighed and continued her narrative. "My human jailers were like the Communities in their attitude toward suicide," she said. "They watched too as I tried to kill myself. I found out later that there were at least three cameras on me day and night. A lab rat had more privacy than I did. They watched me make a noose of my clothing. They watched me climb onto my bed and tie off the noose to a grill that protected the speaker they sometimes used to blast me with loud, distorted music or with old news broadcasts from when the aliens first arrived and people were dying in the panic.

"They even watched me step off my bed and dangle by my neck, strangling. Then they got me out of there, revived me, made sure I wasn't seriously injured. That done, they put me back in my cell, naked and with the speaker recess concreted over and the grill gone. At least, after that there was no more horrible music. No more terrified screaming.

"But the questioning began again. They even said I hadn't really meant to kill myself, that I was just making a bid for sympathy.

"So I left in mind, if not in body. I sort of went catatonic for a while. I wasn't entirely unconscious, but I wasn't functioning any more. I couldn't. They knocked me around at first because they thought I was faking. I know they did that because later I had some unexplained and untreated broken bones and other medical problems to deal with.

"Then someone leaked my story. I don't know who. Maybe one of my interrogators finally grew a conscience. Anyway, someone started telling the media about me and showing them pictures. The fact that I was only eleven when I was taken turned out to be important to the story. At that point, my captors decided to give me up. I suppose they could have killed me just as easily. Considering what they had been doing to me, I have no idea why they didn't kill me. I've seen the pictures that got published. I was in bad shape. Maybe they thought I'd die—or at least that I'd never wake all the way up and be normal again. And, too, once my relatives learned that I was alive, they got lawyers and fought to get me out of there.

"My parents were dead—had died in a car wreck while I was still a captive in the Mojave Bubble. My jailers must have known, but they never said a word. I didn't find out until I began to recover and one of my uncles told me. My uncles were my mother's three older brothers. They were the ones who fought for me. To get me, they had to sign away any rights they may have had to sue. They were told that the Communities were the ones who had injured me. They believed it until I revived enough to tell them what really happened.

"After I told them, they wanted to tell the world, maybe put a few people in prison where they belonged. If they hadn't had families of their own, I might not have been able to talk them out of it. They were good men. My mother was their baby sister, and they'd always loved her and looked after her. As things were, though, they had had to go into serious debt to get me free, repaired and functional again. I couldn't have lived with the thought that because of me, they lost everything they owned, and maybe even got sent to prison on some fake charge.

"When I'd recovered a little, I had to do some media interviews. I told lies, of course, but I couldn't go along with the big lie. I refused to confirm that the Communities had injured me. I pretended not to remember what had happened. I said I had been in such bad shape that I didn't have any idea what was going on most of the time, and that I was just grateful to be free and healing. I hoped that was enough to keep my human ex-captors content. It seemed to be.

"The reporters wanted to know what I was going to do, now that I was free.

"I told them I would go to school as soon as I could. I would get an education, then a job so that I could begin to pay my uncles back for all they had done for me.

"That's pretty much what I did. And while I was in school, I realized what work I was best fitted to do. So here I am. I was not only the first to leave the Mojave Bubble, but the first to come back to offer to work for the Communities. I had a small part in helping them connect with some of the lawyers and politicians I mentioned earlier."

"Did you tell your story to the weeds when you came back here?" Thera Collier asked suspiciously. "Prison and torture and everything?"

Noah nodded. "I did. Some Communities asked and I told them. Most didn't ask. They have problems enough among themselves. What humans do to other humans outside their bubbles is usually not that important to them."

"Do they trust you?" Thera asked. "Do the weeds trust you?"

Noah smiled unhappily. "At least as much as you do, Ms. Collier."

Thera gave a short bark of laughter, and Noah realized the woman had not understood. She thought Noah was only being sarcastic.

"I mean they trust me to do my job," Noah said. "They trust me to help would-be employers learn to live with a human being without hurting the human and to help human employees learn to live with the Communities and fulfill their responsibilities. You trust me to do that too. That's why you're here." That was all true enough, but there were also some Communities—her employer and a few others—who did seem to trust her. And she trusted them. She had never dared to tell anyone that she thought of these as friends.

Even without that admission, Thera gave her a look that seemed to be made up of equal parts pity and contempt.

"Why did the aliens take you back," James Adio demanded. "You could have been bringing in a gun or a bomb or something. You could have been coming back to get even with them for what they'd done to you."

Noah shook her head. "They would have detected any weapon I could bring in. They let me come back because they knew me and they knew I could be useful to them. I knew I could be useful to us, too. They want more of us. Maybe they even need more of us. Better for everyone if they hire us and pay us instead of snatching us. They can take mineral ores from deeper in the ground than we can reach, and refine them. They've agreed to restrictions on what they take and where they take it. They pay a handsome percentage of their profit to the government in fees and taxes. With all that, they still have plenty of money to hire us."

She changed the subject suddenly. "Once you're in the bubble, learn the language. Make it clear to your employers that you want to learn. Have you all mastered the basic signs?" She looked them over, not liking the silence. Finally she asked, "Has anyone mastered the basic signs?"

Rune Johnsen and Michelle Ota both said, "I have."

Sorrel Trent said, "I learned some of it, but it's hard to remember."

The others said nothing. James Adio began to look defensive. "They come to our world and we have to learn their language," he muttered.

"I'm sure they would learn ours if they could, Mr. Adio," Noah said wearily. "In fact, here at Mojave, they can read English, and even write it—with difficulty. But since they can't hear at all, they never developed a spoken language of any kind. They can only converse with us in the gesture and touch language that some of us and some of them have developed. It takes some getting used to since they have no limbs in common with us. That's why you need to learn it from them, see for yourself how they move and feel the touch-signs on your skin when you're enfolded. But once you learn it, you'll see that it works well for both species."

"They could use computers to speak for them," Thera Collier said. "If their technology isn't up to it, they could buy some of ours."

Noah did not bother to look at her. "Most of you won't be required to learn more than the basic signs," she said. "If you have some urgent need that the basics don't cover, you can write notes. Print in block capital letters. That will usually work. But if you want to move up a paygrade or two and be given work that might actually interest you, learn the language."

"How do you learn," Michelle Ota asked. "Are there classes?"

"No classes. Your employers will teach you if they want you to know—or if you ask. Language lessons are the one thing you can ask for that you can be sure of getting. They're also one of the few things that will get your pay reduced if you're told to learn and you don't. That will be in the contract. They won't care whether you won't or you can't. Either way it's going to cost you."

"Not fair," Piedad said.

Noah shrugged. "It's easier if you have something to do anyway, and easier if you can talk with your employer. You can't bring in radios, televisions, computers, or recordings of any kind. You can bring in a few books—the paper kind—but that's all. Your employers can and will call you at any time, sometimes several times in a day. Your employer might lend you to . . . relatives who haven't hired one of us yet. They might also ignore you for days at a time, and most of you won't be within shouting distance of another human being." Noah paused, stared down at the table. "For the sake of your sanity, go in with projects that will occupy your minds."

Rune said, "I would like to hear your description of our duties. What I read sounded almost impossibly simple."

"It is simple. It's even pleasant once you're used to it. You will be enfolded by your employer or anyone your employer designates. If both you and the Community enfolding you can communicate, you might be asked to explain or discuss some aspect of our culture that the Community either doesn't understand or wants to hear more about. Some of them read our literature, our history, even our news. You may be given puzzles to solve. When you're not enfolded, you may be sent on errands—after you've been inside long enough to be able to find your way around. Your employer might sell your contract to another Community, might even send you to one of the other bubbles. They've agreed not to send you out of the country, and they've agreed that when your contract is up, they'll let you leave by way of the Mojave Bubble—since this is where you'll begin. You won't be injured. There'll be no bio-medical experiments, none of the nastier social experiments that captives endured. You'll receive all the food, water, and shelter that you need to keep you healthy. If you get sick or injured, you have the right to see a human physician. I believe there are two human doctors working here at Mojave now." She paused and James Adio spoke up.

"So what will we be, then?" he demanded. "Whores or house pets?"

Thera Collier made a noise that was almost a sob.

Noah smiled humorlessly. "We're neither, of course. But you'll probably feel as though you're both unless you learn the language. We are one interesting and unexpected thing, though." She paused. "We're an addictive drug." She watched the group and recognized that Rune Johnsen had already known this. And Sorrel Trent had known. The other four were offended and uncertain and shocked.

"This effect proves that humanity and the Communities belong together," Sorrel Trent said. "We're fated to be together. They have so much to teach us."

Everyone ignored her.

"You told us they understood that we were intelligent," Michelle Ota said.

"Of course they understand," Noah said. "But what's important to them is not what they think of our intellect. It's what use we can be to them. That's what they pay us for."

"We're not prostitutes!" Piedad Ruiz said. "We're not! There's no sex in any of this. There can't be. And there are no drugs either. You said so yourself!"

Noah turned to look at her. Piedad didn't listen particularly well, and she lived in terror of prostitution, drug addiction, disease, anything that might harm her or steal her ability to have the family she hoped for. Her two older sisters were already selling themselves on the streets. She hoped to rescue them and herself by getting work with the Communities.

"No sex," Noah agreed. "And we are the drugs. The Communities feel better when they enfold us. We feel better too. I guess that's only fair. The ones among them who are having trouble adjusting to this world are calmed and much improved if they can enfold one of us now and then." She thought for a moment. "I've heard that for human beings, petting a cat lowers our blood pressure. For them, enfolding one of us calms them and eases what translates as a kind of intense biological homesickness."

"We ought to sell them some cats," Thera said. "Neutered cats so they'll have to keep buying them."

"Cats and dogs don't like them," Noah said. "As a matter of fact, cats and dogs won't like you after you've lived in the bubble for a while. They seem to smell something on you that we can't detect. They panic if you go near them. They bite and scratch if you try to handle them. The effect lasts for a month or two. I generally avoid house pets and even farm animals for a couple of months when I go out."

"Is being enveloped anything like being crawled over by insects?" Piedad asked. "I can't stand having things crawl on me."

"It isn't like any experience you've ever had," Noah said. "I can only tell you that it doesn't hurt and it isn't slimy or disgusting in any way. The only problem likely to be triggered by it is claustrophobia. If any of you had been found to be claustrophobic, you would have been culled by now. For the non-claustrophobic, well, we're lucky they need us. It means jobs for a lot of people who wouldn't otherwise have them."

"We're the drug of choice, then?" Rune said. And he smiled.

Noah smiled back. "We are. And they have no history of drug taking, no resistance to it, and apparently no moral problems with it. All of a sudden they're hooked. On us."

James Adio said, "Is this some kind of payback for you, Translator? You hook them on us because of what they did to you."

Noah shook her head. "No payback. Just what I said earlier. Jobs. We get to live, and so do they. I don't need payback."

He gave her a long, solemn look. "I would," he said. "I do. I can't have it, but I want it. They invaded us. They took over."

"God, yes," Noah said. "They've taken over big chunks of the Sahara, the Atacama, the Kalahari the Mojave and just about every other hot, dry wasteland they could find. As far as territory goes, they've taken almost nothing that we need."

"They've still got no right to it," Thera said. "It's ours, not theirs."

"They can't leave," Noah said.

Thera nodded. "Maybe not. But they can die!"

Noah ignored this. "Some day maybe a thousand of years from now, some of them will leave. They'll build and use ships that are part multigenerational and part sleeper. A few Communities stay awake and keep things running. Everyone else sort of hibernates." This was a vast oversimplification of the aliens' travel habits, but it was essentially true. "Some of us might even wind up going with them. It would be one way for the human species to get to the stars."

Sorrel Trent said wistfully, "If we honor them, maybe they will take us to heaven with them."

Noah suppressed an urge to hit the woman. To the others, she said, "The next two years will be as easy or as difficult as you decide to make them. Keep in mind that once the contract is signed, the Communities won't let you go because you're angry with them or because you hate them or even because you try to kill them. And by the way, although I'm sure they can be killed, that's only because I believe anything that's alive can die. I've never seen a dead Community, though. I've seen a couple of them have what you might call internal revolution. The entities of those Communities scattered to join other Communities. I'm not sure whether that was death, reproduction, or both." She took a deep breath and let it out. "Even those of us who can talk fluently with the Communities don't understand their physiology that well."

"Finally, I want to tell you a bit of history. When I've done that, I'll I escort you in and introduce you to your employers."

"Are we all accepted, then?" Rune Johnsen asked.

"Probably not," Noah said. "There's a final test. When

you go in, you will be enfolded, each of you, by a potential employer. When that's over, some of you will be offered a contract and the rest will be given the thanks-for-stopping-by fee that anyone who gets this far and no farther is given."

"I had no idea the . . . enfolding . . . would happen so soon," Rune Johnsen said. "Any pointers?"

"About being enfolded?" Noah shook her head. "None. It's a good test. It lets you know whether you can stand the Communities and lets them know whether they really want you."

Piedad Ruiz said, "You were going to tell us something—something from history."

"Yes." Noah leaned back in her chair. "It isn't common knowledge. I looked for references to it while I was in school, but I never found any. Only my military captors and the aliens seemed to know about it. The aliens told me before they let me go. My military captors gave me absolute hell for knowing.

"It seems that there was a coordinated nuclear strike at the aliens when it was clear where they were establishing their colonies. The armed forces of several countries had tried and failed to knock them out of the sky before they landed. Everyone knows that. But once the Communities established their bubbles, they tried again. I was already a captive inside the Mojave bubble when the attack came. I have no idea how that attack was repelled, but I do know this, and my military captors confirmed it with their lines of questioning: the missiles fired at the bubbles never detonated. They should have, but they didn't. And sometime later, exactly half of the missiles that had been fired were returned. They were discovered armed and intact, scattered around Washington DC in the White House—

one in the Oval Office—in the capitol, in the Pentagon. In China, half of the missiles fired at the Gobi Bubbles were found scattered around Beijing. London and Paris got one half of their missiles back from the Sahara and Australia. There was panic, confusion, fury. After that, though, the "invaders," the "alien weeds" began to become in many languages, our "guests," our "neighbors," and even our "friends."

"Half the nuclear missiles were . . . returned?" Piedad Ruiz whispered.

Noah nodded. "Half, yes."

"What happened to the other half?"

"Apparently, the Communities still have the other half—along with whatever weapons they brought with them and any they've built since they've been here."

Silence. The six looked at one another, then at Noah.

"It was a short, quiet war," Noah said. "We lost."

Thera Collier stared at her bleakly. "But . . . but there must be something we can do, some way to fight."

Noah stood up, pushed her comfortable chair away. "I don't think so," she said. "Your employers are waiting. "Shall we join them?"

Afterword

"Amnesty" was inspired by the things that happened to Doctor Wen Ho Lee of Los Alamos—back in the 1990s when I could still be shocked that a person could have his profession and his freedom taken away and his reputation damaged all without proof that he'd actually done anything wrong. I had no idea how commonplace this kind of thing could become.

The Book of Martha

"It's difficult, isn't it?" God said with a weary smile. "You're truly free for the first time. What could be more difficult than that?"

Martha Bes looked around at the endless grayness that was, along with God, all that she could see. In fear and confusion, she covered her broad black face with her hands. "If only I could wake up," she whispered.

God kept silent but was so palpably, disturbingly present that even in the silence Martha felt rebuked. "Where is this?" she asked, not really wanting to know, not wanting to be dead when she was only forty-three. "Where am I?"

"Here with me," God said.

"Really here?" she asked. "Not at home in bed dreaming? Not locked up in a mental institution? Not . . . not lying dead in a morgue?"

"Here," God said softly. "With me."

After a moment, Martha was able to take her hands from her face and look again at the grayness around her and at God. "This can't be heaven," she said. "There's nothing here, no one here but you."

"Is that all you see?" God asked.

This confused her even more. "Don't you know what I see?" she demanded and then quickly softened her voice. "Don't you know everything?"

God smiled. "No, I outgrew that trick long ago. You can't imagine how boring it was."

This struck Martha as such a human thing to say that her fear diminished a little—although she was still impossibly confused. She had, she remembered, been sitting at her computer, wrapping up one more day's work on her fifth novel. The writing had been going well for a change, and she'd been enjoying it. For hours, she'd been spilling her new story onto paper in that sweet frenzy of creation that she lived for. Finally, she had stopped, turned the computer off, and realized that she felt stiff. Her back hurt. She was hungry and thirsty, and it was almost five A.M. She had worked through the night. Amused in spite of her various aches and pains, she got up and went to the kitchen to find something to eat.

And then she was here, confused and scared. The comfort of her small, disorderly house was gone, and she was standing before this amazing figure who had convinced her at once that he was God—or someone so powerful that he might as well be God. He had work for her to do, he said—work that would mean a great deal to her and to the rest of humankind.

If she had been a little less frightened, she might have laughed. Beyond comic books and bad movies, who said things like that?

"Why," she dared to ask, "do you look like a twice-live-sized, bearded white man?" In fact, seated as he was on his huge thronelike chair, he looked, she thought, like a living version of Michelangelo's Moses, a sculpture that she remembered seeing pictured in her college art-history textbook about twenty years before. Except that God was more fully dressed than Michelangelo's Moses, wearing, from neck to ankles, the kind of long, white robe that she had so often seen in paintings of Christ.

"You see what your life has prepared you to see," God said.

"I want to see what's really here!"

"Do you? What you see is up to you, Martha. Everything is up to you."

She sighed. "Do you mind if I sit down?"

And she was sitting. She did not sit down, but simply found herself sitting in a comfortable armchair that had surely not been there a moment before. Another trick, she thought resentfully—like the grayness, like the giant on his throne, like her own sudden appearance here. Everything was just one more effort to amaze and frighten her. And, of course, it was working. She was amazed and badly frightened. Worse, she disliked the giant for manipulating her, and this frightened her even more. Surely he could read her mind. Surely he would punish . . .

She made herself speak through her fear. "You said you had work for me." She paused, licked her lips, tried to steady her voice. "What do you want me to do?"

He didn't answer at once. He looked at her with what she read as amusement—looked at her long enough to make her even more uncomfortable.

"What do you want me to do?" she repeated, her voice stronger this time.

"I have a great deal of work for you," he said at last. "As I tell you about it, I want you to keep three people in mind: Jonah, Job, and Noah. Remember them. Be guided by their stories."

"All right," she said because he had stopped speaking, and it seemed that she should say something. "All right."

When she was a girl, she had gone to church and to Sunday

School, to Bible class and to vacation Bible school. Her mother, only a girl herself, hadn't known much about being a mother, but she had wanted her child to be "good," and to her, "good" meant "religious." As a result, Martha knew very well what the Bible said about Jonah, Job, and Noah. She had come to regard their stories as parables rather than literal truths, but she remembered them. God had ordered Jonah to go to the city of Nineveh and to tell the people there to mend their ways. Frightened, Jonah had tried to run away from the work and from God, but God had caused him to be shipwrecked, swallowed by a great fish, and given to know that he could not escape.

Job had been the tormented pawn who lost his property, his children, and his health, in a bet between God and Satan. And when Job proved faithful in spite of all that God had permitted Satan to do to him, God rewarded Job with even greater wealth, new children, and restored health.

As for Noah, of course, God ordered him to build an ark and save his family and a lot of animals because God had decided to flood the world and kill everyone and everything else.

Why was she to remember these three Biblical figures in particular? What had they do with her—especially Job and all his agony?

"This is what you're to do," God said. "You will help humankind to survive its greedy, murderous, wasteful adolescence. Help it to find less destructive, more peaceful, sustainable ways to live."

Martha stared at him. After a while, she said feebly, ". . . what?"

"If you don't help them, they will be destroyed."

"You're going to destroy them . . . again?" she whispered.

"Of course not," God said, sounding annoyed. "They're well on the way to destroying billions of themselves by greatly changing the ability of the earth to sustain them. That's why they need help. That's why you will help them."

"How?" she asked. She shook her head. "What can I do?"

"Don't worry," God said. "I won't be sending you back home with another message that people can ignore or twist to suit themselves. It's too late for that kind of thing anyway." God shifted on his throne and looked at her with his head cocked to one side. "You'll borrow some of my power," he said. "You'll arrange it so that people treat one another better and treat their environment more sensibly. You'll give them a better chance to survive than they've given themselves. I'll lend you the power, and you'll do this." He paused, but this time she could think of nothing to say. After a while, he went on.

"When you've finished your work, you'll go back and live among them again as one of their lowliest. You're the one who will decide what that will mean, but whatever you decide is to be the bottom level of society, the lowest class or caste or race, that's what you'll be."

This time when he stopped talking, Martha laughed. She felt overwhelmed with questions, fears, and bitter laughter, but it was the laughter that broke free. She needed to laugh. It gave her strength somehow.

"I was born on the bottom level of society," she said. "You must have known that."

God did not answer.

"Sure you did." Martha stopped laughing and managed, somehow, not to cry. She stood up, stepped toward God. "How could you not know? I was born poor, black, and female to a fourteen-year-old mother who could barely read. We were homeless half the time while I was growing up. Is that bottom-level enough for you? I was born on the bottom, but I didn't stay there. I didn't leave my mother there, either. And I'm not going back there!"

Still God said nothing. He smiled.

Martha sat down again, frightened by the smile, aware that she had been shouting—shouting at God! After a while, she whispered, "Is that why you chose me to do this . . . this work? Because of where I came from?"

"I chose you for all that you are and all that you are not," God said. "I could have chosen someone much poorer and more downtrodden. I chose you because you were the one I wanted for this."

Martha couldn't decide whether he sounded annoyed. She couldn't decide whether it was an honor to be chosen to do a job so huge, so poorly defined, so impossible.

"Please let me go home," she whispered. She was instantly ashamed of herself. She was begging, sounding pitiful, humiliating herself. Yet these were the most honest words she'd spoken so far.

"You're free to ask me questions," God said as though he hadn't heard her plea at all. "You're free to argue and think and investigate all of human history for ideas and warnings. You're free to take all the time you need to do these things. As I said earlier, you're truly free. You're even free to be terrified. But I assure you, you will do this work."

Martha thought of Job, Jonah, and Noah. After a while, she nodded.

"Good," God said. He stood up and stepped toward her. He was at least twelve feet high and inhumanly beautiful. He literally glowed. "Walk with me," he said.

And abruptly, he was not twelve feet high. Martha never saw him change, but now he was her size—just under six feet—and he no longer glowed. Now when he looked at her, they were eye to eye. He did look at her. He saw that something was disturbing her, and he asked, "What is it now? Has your image of me grown feathered wings or a blinding halo?"

"Your halo's gone," she answered. "And you're smaller. More normal."

"Good," he said. "What else do you see?"

"Nothing. Grayness."

"That will change."

It seemed that they walked over a smooth, hard, level surface, although when she looked down, she couldn't see her feet. It was as though she walked through ankle-high, ground-hugging fog.

"What are we walking on?" she asked.

"What would you like?" God asked. "A sidewalk? Beach sand? A dirt road?"

"A healthy, green lawn," she said, and was somehow not surprised to find herself walking on short, green grass. "And there should be trees," she said, getting the idea and discovering she liked it. "There should be sunshine—blue sky with a few clouds. It should be May or early June."

And it was so. It was as though it had always been so. They were walking through what could have been a vast city park.

Martha looked at God, her eyes wide. "Is that it?" she whispered. "I'm supposed to change people by deciding what they'll be like, and then just . . . just saying it?"

"Yes," God said.

And she went from being elated to—once again—being terrified. "What if I say something wrong, make a mistake?"

"You will."

"But . . . people could get hurt. People could die."

God went to a huge deep red Norway Maple tree and sat down beneath it on a long wooden bench. Martha realized that he had created both the ancient tree and the comfortable-looking bench only a moment before. She knew this, but again, it had happened so smoothly that she was not jarred by it.

"It's so easy," she said. "Is it always this easy for you?"

God sighed. "Always," he said.

She thought about that—his sigh, the fact that he looked away into the trees instead of at her. Was an eternity of absolute ease just another name for hell? Or was that just the most sacrilegious thought she'd had so far? She said, "I don't want to hurt people. Not even by accident."

God turned away from the trees, looked at her for several seconds, then said, "It would be better for you if you had raised a child or two."

Then, she thought with irritation, he should have chosen someone who'd raised a child or two. But she didn't have the courage to say that. Instead, she said, "Won't you fix it so I don't hurt or kill anyone? I mean, I'm new at this. I could do something stupid and wipe people out and not even know I'd done it until afterward."

"I won't fix things for you," God said. "You have a free hand."

She sat down next to him because sitting and staring out into the endless park was easier than standing and facing him and asking him questions that she thought might make him angry. She said, "Why should it be my work? Why don't you do it? You know how. You could do it without making mistakes. Why make me do it? I don't know anything."

"Quite right," God said. And he smiled. "That's why."

She thought about this with growing horror. "Is it just a game to you, then?" she asked. "Are you playing with us because you're bored?"

God seemed to consider the question. "I'm not bored," he said. He seemed pleased somehow. "You should be thinking about the changes you'll make. We can talk about them. You don't have to just suddenly proclaim."

She looked at him, then stared down at the grass, trying to get her thoughts in order. "Okay. How do I start?"

"Think about this: What change would you want to make if you could make only one? Think of one important change."

She looked at the grass again and thought about the novels she had written. What if she were going to write a novel in which human beings had to be changed in only one positive way? "Well," she said after a while, "the growing population is making a lot of the other problems worse. What if people could only have two children? I mean, what if people who wanted children could only have two, no matter how many more they wanted or how many medical techniques they used to try to get more?"

"You believe the population problem is the worst one, then?" God asked.

"I think so," she said. "Too many people. If we solve that one, we'll have more time to solve other problems. And we can't solve it on our own. We all know about it, but some of us won't admit it. And nobody wants some big government authority telling them how many kids to have." She glanced at God and saw that he seemed to be listening politely. She wondered how far he would let her go. What might offend him. What might he do to her if he were offended? "So everyone's reproductive system shuts down after two kids," she said. "I mean, they get to live as long as before, and they aren't sick. They just can't have kids any more."

"They'll try," God said. "The effort they put into building pyramids, cathedrals, and moon rockets will be as nothing to the effort they'll put into trying to end what will seem to them a plague of barrenness. What about people whose children die or are seriously disabled? What about a woman who's first child is a result of rape? What about surrogate motherhood? What about men who become fathers without realizing it? What about cloning?"

Martha stared at him, chagrined. "That's why you should do this. It's too complicated."

Silence.

"All right," Martha sighed and gave up. "All right. What if even with accidents and modern medicine, even something like cloning, the two-kid limit holds. I don't know how that could be made to work, but you do."

"It could be made to work," God said, "but keep in mind that you won't be coming here again to repair any changes you make. What you do is what people will live with. Or in this case, die with."

"Oh," Martha said. She thought for a moment, then said, "Oh, no."

"They would last for a good many generations," God said. "But they would be dwindling all the time. In the end, they would be extinguished. With the usual diseases, disabilities, disasters, wars, deliberate childlessness, and murder, they wouldn't be able to replace themselves. Think of the needs of the future, Martha, as well as the needs of the present."

"I thought I was," she said. "What if I made four kids the maximum number instead of two?"

God shook his head. "Free will coupled with morality has been an interesting experiment. Free will is, among other things, the freedom to make mistakes. One group of mistakes will sometimes cancel another. That's saved any number of human groups, although it isn't dependable. Sometimes mistakes cause people to be wiped out, enslaved, or driven from their homes because they've so damaged or altered their land or their water or their climate. Free will isn't a guarantee of anything, but it's a potentially useful tool—too useful to erase casually."

"I thought you wanted me to put a stop to war and slavery and environmental destruction!" Martha snapped, remembering the history of her own people. How could God be so casual about such things?

God laughed. It was a startling sound—deep, full, and, Martha thought, inappropriately happy. Why would this particular subject make him laugh? Was he God? Was he Satan? Martha, in spite of her mother's efforts, had not been able to believe in the literal existence of either. Now, she did not know what to think—or what to do.

God recovered himself, shook his head, and looked at Martha. "Well, there's no hurry," he said. "Do you know what a nova is Martha?"

Martha frowned. "It's . . . a star that explodes," she said, willing, even eager, to be distracted from her doubts.

"It's a pair of stars," God said. "A large one—a giant—and a small, very dense dwarf. The dwarf pulls material from the giant. After a while, the dwarf has taken more material than it can control, and it explodes. It doesn't necessarily destroy itself, but it does throw off a great deal of excess material. It makes a very bright, violent display. But once the dwarf has quieted down, it begins to siphon material from the giant again. It can do this over and over. That's what a nova is. If you change it—move the two stars farther apart or equalize their density, then it's no longer a nova."

Martha listened, catching his meaning even though she didn't want to. "Are you saying that if . . . if humanity is changed, it won't be humanity any more?"

"I'm saying more than that," God told her. "I'm saying that even though this is true, I will permit you to do it. What you decide should be done with humankind will be done. But whatever you do, your decisions will have consequences. If you limit their fertility, you will probably destroy them. If you limit their competitiveness or their inventiveness, you might destroy their ability to survive the many disasters and challenges that they must face."

Worse and worse, Martha thought, and she actually felt nauseous with fear. She turned away from God, hugging herself, suddenly crying, tears streaming down her face. After a while, she sniffed and wiped her face on her hands, since she had nothing else. "What will you do to me if I refuse?" she asked, thinking of Job and Jonah in particular.

"Nothing." God didn't even sound annoyed. "You won't refuse."

"But what if I do? What if I really can't think of anything worth doing?"

"That won't happen. But if it did somehow, and if you asked, I would send you home. After all, there are millions of human beings who would give anything to do this work."

And, instantly, she thought of some of these—people who would be happy to wipe out whole segments of the population whom they hated and feared, or people who would set up vast tyrannies that forced everyone into a single mold, no matter how much suffering that created. And what about those who would treat the work as fun—as nothing more than a good-guys-versus-bad-guys computer game, and damn the consequences. There were people like that. Martha knew people like that.

But God wouldn't choose that kind of person. If he was God. Why had he chosen her, after all? For all of her adult life, she hadn't even believed in God as a literal being. If this terrifyingly powerful entity, God or not, could choose her, he could make even worse choices.

After a while, she asked, "Was there really a Noah?"

"Not one man dealing with a worldwide flood," God said. "But there have been a number of people who've had to deal with smaller disasters."

"People you ordered to save a few and let the rest die?"

"Yes," God said.

She shuddered and turned to face him again. "And what then? Did they go mad?" Even she could hear the disapproval and disgust in her voice.

God chose to hear the question as only a question. "Some took refuge in madness, some in drunkenness, some in sexual license. Some killed themselves. Some survived and lived long, fruitful lives."

Martha shook her head and managed to keep quiet.

"I don't do that any longer," God said.

No, Martha thought. Now he had found a different amusement. "How big a change do I have to make?" she asked. "What will please you and cause you to let me go and not bring in someone else to replace me?"

"I don't know," God said, and he smiled. He rested his head back against the tree. "Because I don't know what you will do. That's a lovely sensation—anticipating, not knowing."

"Not from my point of view," Martha said bitterly. After a while, she said in a different tone, "Definitely not from my point of view. Because I don't know what to do. I really don't."

"You write stories for a living," God said. "You create characters and situations, problems and solutions. That's less than I've given you to do."

"But you want me to tamper with real people. I don't want do that. I'm afraid I'll make some horrible mistake."

"I'll answer your questions," God said. "Ask."

She didn't want to ask. After a while, though, she gave in. "What, exactly, do you want? A utopia? Because I don't believe in them. I don't believe it's possible to arrange a society so that everyone is content, everyone has what he or she wants."

"Not for more than a few moments," God said. "That's how long it would take for someone to decide that he wanted what his neighbor had—or that he wanted his neighbor as a slave of one kind or another, or that he wanted his neighbor dead. But never mind. I'm not asking you to create a utopia, Martha, although it would be interesting to see what you could come up with."

"So what are you asking me to do?"

"To help them, of course. Haven't you wanted to do that?"

"Always," she said. "And I never could in any meaningful way. Famines, epidemics, floods, fires, greed, slavery, revenge, stupid, stupid wars . . ."

"Now you can. Of course, you can't put an end to all of those things without putting an end to humanity, but you can diminish some of the problems. Fewer wars, less covetousness, more forethought and care with the environment. . . . What might cause that?"

She looked at her hands, then at him. Something had occurred to her as he spoke, but it seemed both too simple and too fantastic, and to her personally, perhaps, too painful. Could it be done? Should it be done? Would it really help if it were done? She asked, "Was there really anything like the Tower of Babel? Did you make people suddenly unable to understand each other?"

God nodded. "Again, it happened several times in one way or another."

"So what did you do? Change their thinking somehow, alter their memories?"

"Yes, I've done both. Although before literacy, all I had to do was divide them physically, send one group to a new land or give one group a custom that altered their mouths—knocking out the front teeth during puberty rites, for instance. Or give them a strong aversion to something others of their kind consider precious or sacred or—"

To her amazement, Martha interrupted him. "What about changing people's . . . I don't know, their brain activity. Can I do that?"

"Interesting," God said. "And probably dangerous. But you can do that if you decide to. What do you have in mind?"

"Dreams," she said. "Powerful, unavoidable, realistic dreams that come every time people sleep."

"Do you mean," God asked, "that they should be taught some lesson through their dreams?"

"Maybe. But I really mean that somehow people should spend a lot of their energy in their dreams. They would have their own personal best of all possible worlds during their dreams. The dreams should be much more realistic and intense than most dreams are now. Whatever people love to do most, they should dream about doing it, and the dreams should change to keep up with their individual interests. Whatever grabs their attention, whatever they desire, they can have it in their sleep. In fact, they can't avoid having it. Nothing should be able to keep the dreams away—not drugs, not surgery, not anything. And the dreams should satisfy much more deeply, more thoroughly, than reality can. I mean, the satisfaction should be in the dreaming, not in trying to make the dream real."

God smiled. "Why?"

"I want them to have the only possible utopia." Martha thought for a moment. "Each person will have a private, perfect utopia every night—or an imperfect one. If they crave conflict and struggle, they get that. If they want peace and love, they get that. Whatever they want or need comes to them. I think if people go to a . . . well, a private heaven every night, it might take the edge off their willingness to spend their waking hours trying to dominate or destroy one another." She hesitated. "Won't it?"

God was still smiling. "It might. Some people will be taken over by it as though it were an addictive drug. Some will try to fight it in themselves or others. Some will give up on their lives and decide to die because nothing they do matters as much as their dreams. Some will enjoy it and try to go on with their familiar lives, but even they will find that the dreams interfere with their relations with other people. What will humankind in general do? I don't know." He seemed interested, almost excited. "I think it might dull them too much at first—until they're used to it. I wonder whether they can get used to it."

Martha nodded. "I think you're right about it dulling

them. I think at first most people will lose interest in a lot of other things—including real, wide-awake sex. Real sex is risky to both the health and the ego. Dream sex will be fantastic and not risky at all. Fewer children will be born for a while."

"And fewer of those will survive," God said.

"What?"

"Some parents will certainly be too involved in dreams to take care of their children. Loving and raising children is risky, too, and it's hard work.

"That shouldn't happen. Taking care of their kids should be the one thing that parents want to do for real in spite of the dreams. I don't want to be responsible for a lot of neglected kids."

"So you want people—adults and children—to have nights filled with vivid, wish-fulfilling dreams, but parents should somehow see child care as more important than the dreams, and the children should not be seduced away from their parents by the dreams, but should want and need a relationship with them as though there were no dreams?"

"As much as possible." Martha frowned, imagining what it might be like to live in such a world. Would people still read books? Perhaps they would to feed their dreams. Would she still be able to write books? Would she want to? What would happen to her if the only work she had ever cared for was lost? "People should still care about their families and their work," she said. "The dreams shouldn't take away their self-respect. They shouldn't be content to dream on a park bench or in an alley. I just want the dreams to slow things down a little. A little less aggression, as you said, less covetousness. Nothing slows people down like satisfaction, and this satisfaction will come every night."

God nodded. "Is that it, then? Do you want this to happen."

"Yes. I mean, I think so."

"Are you sure?"

She stood up and looked down at him. "Is it what I should do? Will it work? Please tell me."

"I truly don't know. I don't want to know. I want to watch it all unfold. I've used dreams before, you know, but not like this."

His pleasure was so obvious that she almost took the whole idea back. He seemed able to be amused by terrible things. "Let me think about this," she said. "Can I be by myself for a while?"

God nodded. "Speak aloud to me when you want to talk. I'll come to you."

And she was alone. She was alone inside what looked and felt like her home—her little house in Seattle, Washington. She was in her living room.

Without thinking, she turned on a lamp and stood looking at her books. Three of the walls of the room were covered with bookshelves. Her books were there in their familiar order. She picked up several, one after another—history, medicine, religion, art, crime. She opened them to see that they were, indeed her books, highlighted and written in by her own hand as she researched this novel or that short story.

She began to believe she really was at home. She had had some sort of strange waking dream about meeting with a God who looked like Michelangelo's Moses and who ordered her to come up with a way to make humanity a less self-destructive species. The experience felt completely, unnervingly real, but it couldn't have been. It was too ridiculous.

She went to her front window and opened the drapes. Her house was on a hill and faced east. Its great luxury was that it offered a beautiful view of Lake Washington just a few blocks down the hill.

But now, there was no lake. Outside was the park that she had wished into existence earlier. Perhaps twenty yards from her front window was the big red Norway maple tree and the bench where she had sat and talked with God.

The bench was empty now and in deep shadow. It was getting dark outside.

She closed the drapes and looked at the lamp that lit the room. For a moment, it bothered her that it was on and using electricity in this Twilight Zone of a place. Had her house been transported here, or had it been duplicated? Or was it all a complex hallucination?

She sighed. The lamp worked. Best to just accept it. There was light in the room. There was a room, a house. How it all worked was the least of her problems.

She went to the kitchen and there found all the food she had had at home. Like the lamp, the refrigerator, the electric stovetop, and the ovens worked. She could prepare a meal. It would be at least as real as anything else she'd run across recently. And she was hungry.

She took a small can of solid white albacore tuna and containers of dill weed and curry power from the cupboard and got bread, lettuce, dill pickles, green onions, mayonnaise, and chunky salsa from the refrigerator. She would have a tuna-salad sandwich or two. Thinking about it made her even hungrier.

Then she had another thought, and she said aloud, "May I ask you a question?"

And they were walking together on a broad, level dirt pathway bordered by dark, ghostly silhouettes of trees. Night had fallen, and the darkness beneath the trees was impenetrable. Only the pathway was a ribbon of pale light—starlight and moonlight.

There was a full moon, brilliant, yellow-white, and huge. And there was a vast canopy of stars. She had seen the night sky this way only a few times in her life. She had always lived in cities where the lights and the smog obscured all but the brightest few stars.

She looked upward for several seconds, then looked at God and saw, somehow, without surprise, that he was black now, and clean-shaven. He was a tall, stocky black man wearing ordinary, modern clothing—a dark sweater over a white shirt and dark pants. He didn't tower over her, but he was taller than the human-sized version of the white God had been. He didn't look anything like the white Moses-God, and yet he was the same person. She never doubted that.

"You're seeing something different," God said. "What is it?" Even his voice was changed, deepened.

She told him what she was seeing, and he nodded. "At some point, you'll probably decide to see me as a woman," he said.

"I didn't decide to do this," she said. "None of it is real, anyway."

"I've told you," he said. "Everything is real. It's just not as you see it."

She shrugged. It didn't matter—not compared to what she wanted to ask. "I had a thought," she said, "and it scared me. That's why I called you. I sort of asked about it before, but you didn't give me a direct answer, and I guess I need one."

He waited.

"Am I dead?"

"Of course not," he said, smiling. "You're here."

"With you," she said bitterly.

Silence.

"Does it matter how long I take to decide what to do?"

"I've told you, no. Take as long as you like."

That was odd, Martha thought. Well, everything was odd. On impulse, she said, "Would you like a tuna-salad sandwich?"

"Yes," God said. "Thank you."

They walked back to the house together instead of simply appearing there. Martha was grateful for that. Once inside, she left him sitting in her living room, paging through a fantasy novel and smiling. She went through the motions of making the best tuna-salad sandwiches she could. Maybe effort counted. She didn't believe for a moment that she was preparing real food or that she and God were going to eat it.

And yet, the sandwiches were delicious. As they ate, Martha remembered the sparkling apple cider that she kept in the refrigerator for company. She went to get it, and when she got back to the living room, she saw that God had, in fact, become a woman.

Martha stopped, startled, then sighed. "I see you as female now," she said. "Actually, I think you look a little like me. We look like sisters." She smiled wearily and handed over a glass of cider.

God said, "You really are doing this yourself, you know. But as long as it isn't upsetting you, I suppose it doesn't matter."

"It does bother me. If I'm doing it, why did it take so long for me to see you as a black woman—since that's no more true than seeing you as a white or a black man?"

"As I've told you, you see what your life has prepared you to see." God looked at her, and for a moment, Martha felt that she was looking into a mirror.

Martha looked away. "I believe you. I just thought I had already broken out of the mental cage I was born and raised in—a human God, a white God, a male God . . ."

"If it were truly a cage," God said, "you would still be in it, and I would still look the way I did when you first saw me."

"There is that," Martha said. "What would you call it then?"

"An old habit," God said. "That's the trouble with habits. They tend to outlive their usefulness."

Martha was quiet for a while. Finally she said, "What do you think about my dream idea? I'm not asking you to foresee the future. Just find fault. Punch holes. Warn me."

God rested her head against the back of the chair. "Well, the evolving environmental problems will be less likely to cause wars, so there will probably be less starvation, less disease. Real power will be less satisfying than the vast, absolute power they can possess in their dreams, so fewer people will be driven to try to conquer their neighbors or exterminate their minorities. All in all, the dreams will probably give humanity more time than it would have without them.

Martha was alarmed in spite of herself. "Time to do what?"

"Time to grow up a little. Or at least, time to find some way of surviving what remains of its adolescence." God smiled. "How many times have you wondered how some especially self-destructive individual managed to survive adolescence? It's a valid concern for humanity as well as for individual human beings."

"Why can't the dreams do more than that?" she asked. "Why can't the dreams be used not just to give them their heart's desire when they sleep, but to push them toward some kind of waking maturity. Although I'm not sure what species maturity might be like."

"Exhaust them with pleasure," God mused, "while teaching them that pleasure isn't everything."

"They already know that."

"Individuals usually know that by the time they reach adulthood. But all too often, they don't care. It's too easy to follow bad but attractive leaders, embrace pleasurable but destructive habits, ignore looming disaster because maybe it won't happen after all—or maybe it will only happen to other people. That kind of thinking is part of what it means to be adolescent."

"Can the dreams teach—or at least promote—more thoughtfulness when people are awake, promote more concern for real consequences?

"It can be that way if you like."

"I do. I want them to enjoy themselves as much as they can while they're asleep, but to be a lot more awake and aware when they are awake, a lot less susceptible to lies, peer pressure, and self-delusion."

"None of this will make them perfect, Martha."

Martha stood looking down at God, fearing that she had missed something important, and that God knew it and was amused. "But this will help?" she said. "It will help more than it will hurt."

"Yes, it will probably do that. And it will no doubt do other things. I don't know what they are, but they are inevitable. Nothing ever works smoothly with humankind."

"You like that, don't you?"

"I didn't at first. They were mine, and I didn't know them. You cannot begin to understand how strange that was." God shook her head. "They were as familiar as my own substance, and yet they weren't."

"Make the dreams happen." Martha said.

"Are you sure?"

"Make them happen."

"You're ready to go home, then."

"Yes."

God stood and faced her. "You want to go. Why?"

"Because I don't find them interesting in the same way you do. Because your ways scare me."

God laughed—a less disturbing laugh now. "No, they don't," she said. "You're beginning to like my ways."

After a time, Martha nodded. "You're right. It did scare me at first, and now it doesn't. I've gotten used to it. In just the short time that I've been here, I've gotten used to it, and I'm starting to like it. That's what scares me."

In mirror image, God nodded, too. "You really could have stayed here, you know. No time would pass for you. No time has passed."

"I wondered why you didn't care about time."

"You'll go back to the life you remember, at first. But soon, I think you'll have to find another way of earning a living. Beginning again at your age won't be easy."

Martha stared at the neat shelves of books on her walls. "Reading will suffer, won't it—pleasure reading, anyway?"

"It will—for a while, anyway. People will read for information and for ideas, but they'll create their own fantasies. Did you think of that before you made your decision?"

Martha sighed. "Yes," she said. "I did." Sometime later, she added, "I want to go home."

"Do you want to remember being here?" God asked.

"No." On impulse, she stepped to God and hugged her—hugged her hard, feeling the familiar woman's body beneath the blue jeans and black T-shirt that looked as though it had come from Martha's own closet. Martha realized that somehow, in spite of everything, she had come to like this seductive, child-like, very dangerous being. "No," she repeated. "I'm afraid of the unintended damage that the dreams might do."

"Even though in the long run they'll almost certainly do more good than harm?" God asked.

"Even so," Martha said. "I'm afraid the time might come when I won't be able to stand knowing that I'm the one who caused not only the harm, but the end of the only career I've ever cared about. I'm afraid knowing all that might drive me out of my mind someday. She stepped away from God, and already God seemed to be fading, becoming translucent, transparent, gone.

"I want to forget," Martha said, and she stood alone in her living room, looking blankly past the open drapes of her front window at the surface of Lake Washington and the mist that hung above it. She wondered at the words she had just spoken, wondered what it was she wanted so badly to forget.

Afterword

"The Book of Martha" is my utopia story. I don't like most utopia stories because I don't believe them for a moment. It seems inevitable that my utopia would be someone else's hell. So, of course, I have God demand of poor Martha that she come up with a utopia that would work. And where else could it work but in everyone's private, individual dreams?